TOMMY'S SUNSET

AsiaWorld

Series Editor: Mark Selden

This series charts the frontiers of Asia in global perspective. Central to its concerns are Asian interactions—political, economic, social, cultural, and historical—that are transnational and global, that cross and redefine borders and networks, including those of nation, region, ethnicity, gender, technology, and demography. It looks to multiple methodologies to chart the dynamics of a region that has been the home to major civilizations and is central to global processes of war, peace, and development in the new millennium.

Titles in the Series

China's Unequal Treaties: Narrating National History, by Dong Wang

The Culture of Fengshui in Korea: An Exploration of East Asian Geomancy, by Hong-Key Yoon

Precious Steppe: Mongolian Nomadic Pastoralists in Pursuit of the Market, by Ole Bruun

Managing God's Higher Learning: U.S.-China Cultural Encounter and Canton Christian College (Lingnan University), 1888–1952, by Dong Wang

Queer Voices from Japan: First Person Narratives from Japan's Sexual Minorities, edited by Mark McLelland, Katsuhiko Suganuma, and James Welker

Yōko Tawada: Voices from Everywhere, edited by Douglas Slaymaker

Modernity and Re-enchantment: Religion in Post-revolutionary Vietnam, edited by Philip Taylor

Water: The Looming Crisis in India, by Binayak Ray

Windows on the Chinese World: Reflections by Five Historians, by Clara Wing-chung Ho

Tommy's Sunset, by Hisako Tsurushima

Lake of Heaven: An original translation of the Japanese novel by Ishimure Michiko, by Bruce Allen

TOMMY'S SUNSET

Hisako Tsurushima

Translated by Mayumi Ishikawa

LEXINGTON BOOKS

A division of
ROWMAN & LITTLEFIELD PUBLISHERS, INC.
Lanham • Boulder • New York • Toronto • Plymouth, UK

LEXINGTON BOOKS

A division of Rowman & Littlefield Publishers, Inc.
A wholly owned subsidiary of The Rowman & Littlefield Publishing Group, Inc.
4501 Forbes Boulevard, Suite 200
Lanham, MD 20706

Estover Road
Plymouth PL6 7PY
United Kingdom

British Library Cataloguing in Publication Information Available

Library of Congress Cataloging-in-Publication Data

Tsurushima, Hisako, 1934–
  [Tomi no yūhi. English]
  Tommy's sunset / Hisako Tsurushima ; translated by Mayumi Ishikawa.
    p. cm. — (Asia world)
  ISBN-13: 978-0-7391-2405-5 (cloth : alk. paper)
  ISBN-10: 0-7391-2405-6 (cloth : alk. paper)
  ISBN-13: 978-0-7391-2406-2 (pbk. : alk. paper)
  ISBN-10: 0-7391-2406-4 (pbk. : alk. paper)
  ISBN-13: 978-0-7391-3061-2 (electronic)
  ISBN-10: 0-7391-3061-7 (electronic)
  I. Ishikawa, Mayumi. II. Title.
  PL862.S756T6613 2008
  895.6'35—dc22   2008026610

Printed in the United States of America

♾™ The paper used in this publication meets the minimum requirements of American National Standard for Information Sciences—Permanence of Paper for Printed Library Materials, ANSI/NISO Z39.48–1992.

CONTENTS

FOREWORD

I was warming up for a third installment of my *Gakko* [School] series when I saw a TV documentary titled *Our Fresh Start*. In it middle-aged and older men who had lost their full-time jobs thanks to corporate restructuring or bankruptcy were taking lessons at a vocational training center. Thus I came to know that there are indeed publicly run vocational centers all over Japan. They are schools where you can be trained to work as, say, a gardener or a building custodian—rather quiet jobs that may be particularly suitable for elderly people. Here is another form of *gakko*, I thought. This could be the setting for the movie, *Gakko III*.

But when I got down to writing the script, I found that it lacked a core around which everything else in the film would crystallize. Then I remembered reading Hisako Tsurushima's novel *Tommy's Sunset*. It is a wonderful novel about her autistic son who appears in it as Tommy, the protagonist and the narrator. Just marvelous. The writing is lively, crisp, and so humorous as to make you laugh despite your self. The book could be made into a movie that would be bright and poignant at the same time.

Wait a minute, I said. What if I tuck this into *Gakko III*? I had been toying with ideas for a love story in it. Suppose the mother becomes unemployed and enrolls in the training center. Tommy is the key person in her life. Let's make him the core. Around him gather his mom, a man in love with her, and a number of old guys, friends who gently watch over them. Yes, now the plot was starting to take shape.

I had already made forty-eight films in the *Tora-san* series. Tora-san, a kind-hearted vagabond who travels Japan peddling his wares, is always unlucky in love, and always getting into trouble. But what about his position in his hometown, Shibamata, Tokyo? Sometimes he is laughed at, sometimes he raises eyebrows. What if someone said, "He's an embarrassment. Throw him out!" The town folks would surely answer, "Yes, he may be a big troublemaker. But still, he is one of us. You have no right to banish him from town."

I think that's what society, community, and family are all about. It's the same in school as in society as a whole. People with their many differences accept those differences and search for a space where they can cooperate—that's what society is.

The charm of *Tommy's Sunset* resides in its light touch and its humor. No doubt this is in the author's character. One must live positively. Turning back solves nothing. It was with this attitude and strong will working in the background that Hisako Tsurushima was able to write such a work. Anyway, the brightness, the light touch of this novel became the movie's core, and around that, swirled the weighty problems of today's Japan. It became clear to me that in this form, the movie would work. So I sat down and began to write.

Yōji Yamada, film director
from his speech in 1999

ACKNOWLEDGMENTS

Tommy's Sunset was written in Japanese by Hisako Tsurushima and published in 1997 under the title *Tommy no Yūhi*. The six stories narrated by Tommy from the original book were translated into English by Mayumi Ishikawa with contributions by C. Douglas Lummis.

1

FIREWORKS

I never knew the rain could be so warm.

I was deliberately turning my face to the sky to catch the fine raindrops. It puzzled me that occasionally rose-colored drops would trickle into my eyes. Later I learned that the rain had mixed with the blood from the wound on my head.

I sat up in the middle of the road. Dawn was breaking. I put both hands on the road and tried hard to stand up, but both my shoes were gone, and my dangling socks slithered around ineffectually on the cement.

My bike was bent in half, and lay in the street about five meters ahead of me, like an abandoned boomerang. One after another cars and dump trucks stopped, and people got out and gathered around me. Their jaws dropped as they approached me, as if on signal.

The more I felt the need to say something, the more speechless I became. Not only that, I couldn't even begin one of my very own soliloquies, or come up with one of those original questions that only I know how to ask.

Suddenly the layered clouds opened and let through a ray of light, and the morning's first patch of blue sky came into the view. At the same time a familiar smell enveloped me.

"What happened, for . . . ?"

Mom's voice cut off with a quiver.

She bent down over me. Her cheeks were pale and contorted, and I couldn't tell if she was crying or laughing.

An ambulance stopped two cars ahead of us, and two men came running over. They put me in a stretcher.

"Where would you like us to take him, S Hospital, H Hospital, or T Hospital?" the helmeted paramedic asked hurriedly as he got in the ambulance and shut the door.

"Whichever is nearest." The color had returned to Mom's face, and her voice sounded more calm and grave than I had ever heard it.

The speeding ambulance's siren sounded down through the early morning streets.

The usual two extra copies of the newspaper remained in the big box attached to the rear of my bike. The morning delivery round over, I stopped under a telephone pole on the wide street and looked at my wristwatch.

Five twenty; five minutes early. I felt a slight dissatisfaction. Five twenty-*five*, that's what my watch says every morning when I look at it at this point. My eyes strayed across the street to a cluster of vending machines. Suddenly I felt like drinking a cola.

Not that I was especially thirsty. It was that extra five minutes that gave me the idea. When I look at my watch under this telephone pole, it is supposed to say five twenty-five. Then return home by five thirty. When things move along in that way, I can say today has had a perfect beginning.

I turned my bike to cross the still mostly deserted street. Immediately there was a sound like a ripping explosion, and a flashing ball slammed into the side of my bike. It was all over in an instant. I was thrown three meters down the road, and the motorcycle roared on its way.

Strangely, there was no pain.

"Where, what part of your leg? Where does it hurt?"

While the paramedic applied antiseptic to the wound on my head, Mom ran her hands over my legs and asked fragmented questions.

I blurted out, "It doesn't hurt! It doesn't hurt! It doesn't hurt!"

Usually I can't carry on an ordinary conversation, but only say something off the point, and Mom bemoans, "Why are you always saying something irrelevant, you who are already past thirty? It's pitiful!" But this time Mom looked at my face with surprise. I recognized a flicker in her eyes and a motion of her lips that hinted a trace of delight. Even in this situation she was happy not that I wasn't in pain, but that I had given a sensible answer.

"In extreme situations you become a little bit normal." She didn't say it, but I knew that was what she was thinking.

Ordinarily it goes something like this. Mom will say,

"I hate to trouble you, but will you go out and buy some bread and onions?"

And if I don't feel like it I'll go and say something like, "I wonder what day of the week today is. I wonder what day of the week next Monday will be."

For me, this is my best effort to express myself, but for Mom it's only irritating.

If it's just between Mom and me, she is used to me after all these years, and as in the end I agree to go and do the shopping that will settle the matter. But if there are other people around, it's not so simple. Mom gets more hesitant and tries to keep up appearances, so that my endless soliloquy and off-the-wall responses are more likely to get her painted into a corner.

Being basically timid and fainthearted, if I get even a little cut on my finger or even more if I have a stomachache or a headache, I become relatively obedient to Mom's direction, and my speech becomes fairly normal. "In extreme situations you become a little bit normal" is her expression for it.

Some twenty years ago, when I was in the sixth grade, I entered the class of a teacher who was burning with idealism. Several times a week Maeda-sensei would take time after school to play catch with me. He seemed to believe that the game of catch was the origin of all communication, and he wouldn't give it up even in a light rain.

As for me, I would play half-heartedly, catching and returning balls when I didn't have to move to do it, but ignoring the ones that I couldn't catch or that went astray.

"Come on! Can't you get it? What are you doing? Look, the ball's over there!"

He would shout himself hoarse trying to get me to move, and I would have no choice but to drag myself over to where the ball was, muttering all the way.

One day our regular spot was occupied, and we moved to a place alongside the big river. After a few exchanges I saw from the corner of my eye the ball whizzing past me. Traveling at a good speed, the ball landed behind me and began to roll. It was headed for the river.

"Get it! Go after it! It's going to fall into the river!"

Maeda-sensei's big voice jolted me into turning around. I saw the white ball rolling along the bank parallel to the river, about one meter from the water.

In a reflex action, I began to run. I saw the white ball rolling over the green grass and inching closer to the river, as if teasing me. I felt like the ball falling in the water would be like falling in myself. I ran with all my might. This was no time for monologue. Running was all there was in my mind.

Just as the ball reached the water's edge, my hand scooped it up.

"Wo-w!"

I heard Maeda-sensei's voice right behind me.

While my body swayed and my voice failed me, I felt his hands give a squeeze to my shoulders, and his voice rained down on me.

"You can do it if you try! That was great, terrific! This is going to be the source of your new self-confidence. You can do anything!"

Maeda-sensei's passion filled the air, and I enjoyed a moment of euphoria.

I wanted to express my gratitude to him, but all I could come up with was,

"I wonder what class the third period tomorrow will be."

He gave me an "Oh-no-not-that-again" look, but he seemed to be still mesmerized by the fact that I had dashed off to rescue the ball that was about to be lost in the river. So he said,

"That's it. In an extreme situation, you can do it."

That's how he explained it to himself.

And now maybe he was thinking that, using this as a turning point, and with a little more effort, he could teach me how to study, and eventually enable me to mingle smoothly with society.

"Dreamer, dreamer! Don't you realize how many times he's let me down? No, no, this child has absolutely nothing to do with endeavor or success stories"—I could hear Mom's voice in my ears.

And now here I was in the most extreme of extreme situations.

The siren above my head faded out as if it had run out of air. The two medics hurriedly opened the door and carried me out.

Morning sunlight shot into my eyes. The next moment I was swallowed into the dimly lit hallway of the hospital.

The paramedics placed me on a bed under the brilliant illumination of an examination room and then left, Mom along with them. A mix of different sounds came and went by my ears. Then a fair face appeared in front of me. The nurse's smile seemed to say, "Everything will be all right." On her breast were two Chinese characters that I knew how to read, "ice" and "field," which together made the surname "Hino." I was even quick enough in that instant to pinpoint a little mole by the side of her nose.

I heard the snapping sound of scissors on cloth, and then one leg felt cool. Hino-san had cut off the pant leg of my jeans. My leg felt strange, and I couldn't move it.

A big, bearded doctor was standing next to me.

"See if you can sit up."

Following the doctor's words, I sat up.

"The head injury is not serious."

The doctor lightly stroked my pale left leg. To the nurse he said, "X-ray," and to me, "It was a motorcycle, wasn't it? This is going to take some time."

"I don't know what a tanuki road is."

Now that I was calmed down, my regular ways returned. That was my favorite question in those days.

"What?!"

The doctor gave me a perplexed look, and his eyes seemed to have nowhere to go. Then in a stiffened voice, he said,

"Anyway, X-ray."

A door that looked like a sheet hanging sideways swayed open and Mom came tumbling in.

"Ah, well—Doctor, what?—I'm his mother."

The doctor's face relaxed.

"It's going to take some time. Your son has a broken femur and a broken knee. The knee—rather than a compound fracture, I'd say it's been crushed."

Mom caught her breath, and I saw a slight shudder run through her.

Suddenly I was gripped by a fear I had never felt before. I cried out,

"It doesn't hurt! It doesn't hurt! It doesn't hurt!"

I couldn't move my leg, and my whole body felt heavy and enshrouded in mist. There was nothing to do but shout.

The doctor was making it clear that, aside from my injuries, he wanted to know more about me.

Mom had regained some of her composure, but when their eyes met she said, "I'm sorry, Doctor. For him to converse is rather—well, we'll see."

She was uncharacteristically flustered.

"I see. Anyway, let's get the X-ray."

The gurney on which I lay was moved this way and that by Hino and another nurse as they worked around into the X-ray room. I could do nothing but look straight up, and so I watched the shapes and colors on the ceiling and the bright fluorescent lights as they went by. It made me dizzy.

Finally the X-ray was over and I lay with my leg being pulled by weights attached to strings. I couldn't move. I wondered what would happen.

Generally I am not very good at anticipating or thinking about the future. So the only way I have to deal with an anxiety like this one is to search the drawer of my memory, and take out the recollections of all the fears and anxieties I have felt in the past, and line them up. It's like a card game. I try to find a card that matches the card I am now holding. Once I find a match, all my anxiety disappears immediately. No one can equal me in this feat.

I seem to hear Mom's irritated voice, saying,

"You're so simple! You get one idea fixed in your head—like if it's mayonnaise you absolutely only buy Kewpie brand. But the world has other things in it, like Benibana and Ajinomoto."

But we're thinking on different levels. Before I decide that mayonnaise must be Kewpie, how many cards I have taken out from and put back into my memory! It's just that I have never been able to discover the language with which I could explain this to Mom.

But this time I was stuck. There was no card in any of my drawers that can match this anxiety.

"I wonder what day of the week the day after tomorrow will be. I wonder what day of the week today's date last year was. I wonder what would happen if we went home right now."

Words flew out of my mouth one after another.

The stretcher came to a halt. Hino and the other nurse shifted me into a bed.

Where am I? I could feel the presence of others.

A boy of high school age hobbled over to me on crutches. On the bed next to mine a gray-haired man with a newspaper spread out on his lap was looking at me.

Somehow I had an insight. From now, this was going to be my place.

I have a long history of getting hung up on particular things. Especially I am very particular about time and place. And I cannot bear sudden changes in things.

In my elementary school days I would put up fierce resistance against any changes in the class schedule. For example, if the next class was supposed to be science, and I was sitting with my science text and notebook and pencil box all arranged on the desk, and then at the bell the teacher came in and said that for some reason the class would be Japanese or homeroom or something like that—that I couldn't bear. I would burst into tears. It wasn't that I liked science, or that I had actually prepared for the class. It was a feeling of despair, as though some bottomless fear had told me the world was coming to an end.

"What shall we do? Well, shall we follow the original schedule after all? The schedule does say it's science. No wonder Kashiwagi-kun is upset."

The middle-aged teacher was extraordinarily kind. Not only that, she always called me "Kashiwagi-kun," at least in class, while everyone else always called me Tommy, the nickname Mom had concocted from my given name, Tomio.

This thoughtful teacher soon figured out that I would not make a fuss over changes if she told me in advance. So she would tell me in the morning, or use other ways to prevent my being suddenly confronted with changes. But to tell the truth, I would have felt best if I had been told a week in advance.

It's the same with me about place. In my school, class seating was rearranged at the beginning of each semester. So for me this worked the other way: if the seating *wasn't* rearranged I would get upset. And as soon as I sat in my new place I would feel strangely attached to it. This girl in front of me, that boy behind, this girl on the left, that boy on the right. It was soothing to have the new seating confirmed. This is where I would be until the next reseating.

Lying on the white bed, I spotted a brown stain on the ceiling, and made up my mind that this was going to be my place from now.

Then I heard Mom's voice. A nurse had called her out into the hallway. My bed was next to the entrance, so I could clearly hear what they were saying.

"Oh, no. A large room with four to six people would be . . ."

Unusually, Mom's voice sounded inhibited.

"We put him here for the moment, because there happened to be an empty bed. The head nurse told us . . . to avoid inconvenience to the others . . ."

This was the voice of a nurse who was not Hino. Hino had placed a thermometer under my arm and was gently holding it steady with her hand.

If the noises of my neighbor's unfolding newspaper and of the high school boy's jabbering with his visiting friends could be likened to background music, the words spoken by Mom and the nurse in the hall stood out like the two lead actors on a stage—they came into my ears that clearly.

"But you have already put him here."

"The single room is sunny, and it's separated from the larger rooms so it is very quiet."

"His injuries don't seem to be life-threatening. He'll be better off here, where it's livelier."

Mom's voice broke a little. Hang on, Mom! Hang on! I began to get apprehensive.

Compulsively, the words came out of my mouth.

"I don't know what a tanuki road is."

This was my new mantra at that time. I also didn't know the answer to it.

I had meant to ask it to Mom. But Hino, who had put the thermometer in her pocket and was holding my hand to take my pulse, said,

"A tanuki road?"

She tilted her head and asked back,

"Wouldn't that be a road traveled by tanukis? Of course: it would be a wild animal trail, wouldn't it?"

Hino must have known me from long ago. She was my kind of person.

"Well, don't think about things too much. You have to build up strength for your operation. Just try to get some sleep today."

She patted my hand a couple of times and left.

"Please let him stay in the large room. I'll see to it that he isn't a nuisance to the others. Please ask the Director to allow it."

It was Mom's voice from the hall again.

I didn't understand much about the difference between a large room and a single room. But I had only heard Mom talk like that, in that tone of voice, a few times before. It was always at a moment when something was ending or something was beginning in my life. There was only one case when Mom retreated without a word.

I was five. My first term at the childcare center in the Buddhist temple that Mom had persuaded to accept me had ended. Laying out my smock and my pencil box with my crayons and *origami* paper in it on the table in front of Mom and me, the lady said, "It's just impossible. We can't take care of this child. Please try to find another institution that is appropriate for him." From the beginning the Director's wife had spoken in a domineering way so as never to let the other say a word in return. This time too, having delivered her ultimatum, she stood up and walked out the rear of the room, closing the door behind her.

Stunned, Mom sat motionless for a moment, then sprang to her feet, took my hand, went out the door and began walking—fast. She was pulling my hand much harder than usual, so I looked up at her face. She had an angry look like I had never seen before. She seemed to be trying to bear the unbearable.

I was worried about what would happen to the pencil box and the smock we had left behind. Sometimes I also get attached to things.

"What on earth was that? So utterly rude! Treating people as if they weren't human beings! If you have to reject him, there's a way to do it. Are you human? And that Director, afraid to come out himself, and sending out his wife! It's . . ."

Mom's voice faltered and she made sobbing sounds.

"And they call that a temple? And that man is a priest? And Buddha, where is he?"

Her words were mixed with sobs and groans. Her agitation was so great and the power transmitted from her through her hand was so strong that I felt I was just sailing along behind her.

Suddenly the air felt chilly and the edge of the sky began to turn red.

"Ah! Sunset!"

If you ask me what I like, there is nothing in the world I love better than to watch the sun go down. In a world that has turned orange as far as the eye can see, to watch the sun disappear over the edge of the earth leaving rays of light behind—that's the time I feel utter bliss.

That evening was especially gorgeous. There wasn't a speck of cloud in the sky. With a surprising burst of strength I twisted free from Mom's hand and ran toward the setting sun.

"Ah, Tommy! Tommy, wait! Wait for me!"

She came running after me.

We went together up a hill and sat on an embankment facing the setting sun. Little by little the skyline was turning from orange to gray. Strangely, at times like this my monologue would also fade into the shadows.

We sat silently for a while.

Suddenly Mom said in a big voice,

"I paid in advance for the second and third semesters. I want that money back, no matter what!"

I had thought she was watching the sunset with me, but her mind was still filled with what had happened at the childcare center.

"But—ah, I'm sick of it. I don't even want to pass in front of that temple again. Listen, do you realize how much I struggled and worked to get you in there? I went there every morning with you and stayed the whole day taking care of other kids."

She again cried tears of mortification.

Forget about the childcare center. If we can watch the sun go down like this, nothing else matters. I don't need to go to any childcare center.

That's what I was thinking as I watched the last ray of the sun disappear. Without stirring, Mom watched the western sky darken. Blackness fell around us.

"Well, it's ok."

The words fell from her mouth.

"All right, that's the end of it. It makes me mad about the money, though. But then, Tommy was anyway able to go there, even if it was only for one semester. Maybe I'll just donate the money."

"What happens to your pencil box?"

The words flying from my own mouth surprised me. It seems that deep in my heart I still wanted to go there.

"Eh? The box, you're worried about that? Ha, ha, ha! You pick odd places to get commonsensical. But forget about the box. And anyway, you should say 'my box.' Why can't you distinguish between 'I' and 'you'? Ahhh—"

Today, twenty-five years later, it was just the same. The only difference was that Mom was a little tougher, and I was bedridden.

"Please, I am asking you. Please let him stay in the big room."

The nurse fell silent. Mom's tension crunched its way through the wall and traveled into my body. Then the nurse's voice again.

"All right, I'll talk it over with the Head Nurse."

Her voice sounded as though she had just unloaded a big burden from her shoulders.

A little after that, Hino and another nurse came and whisked me off on the bed to a laboratory.

Mom came along with us, looking gloomy.

"I wonder what month and date and day of the week today is," I ventured, thinking to cheer her up.

Hino smiled slightly, and with her eyes sent a message to the other nurse, Nakagawa-san, who looked like a junior high school girl, to answer the question.

"Ahh, this is quite out of the blue," Nakagawa blushed. "It's Thursday, June 20."

She answered as she would have done in a classroom, if asked by a teacher.

The two nurses took a blood sample, measured my blood pressure, and what not. Then an older nurse came in and beckoned to Mom. It was the Head Nurse.

"Kashiwagi-san."

She was speaking to Mom in a corner of the room.

"The fee for a single room is eight thousand yen a day, but we will give it to you for two thousand. So we would like to recommend that he be put in a single room."

Lying flat on my back, still the sound of Mom catching her breath felt frighteningly close.

The Head Nurse pressed on. "It is separated, quiet, and sunny. If necessary we can give it to you for free." She spoke in a low voice, and for a moment I felt uneasy.

"I am very grateful for your concern. But this fellow, though he is as you see, likes people. He can't endure six months in a room alone. And once he gets a cast on his leg, he won't be able to move around by himself. Those youngsters with broken bones seem to be having a merry time in the big rooms, don't they? So—please!"

My unease was completely off the mark. Mom's words came out composed and cool, as though passed through a filter. This time it was the Head Nurse's turn to catch her breath.

Nakagawa was standing straight next to me; I saw her rosy cheeks turn redder still, and her eyes narrow in a slight smile. Hino was doing some work facing the wall.

"I will see to it that there is no inconvenience to the others. I will be very grateful for your consideration."

Before Mom finished, the Head Nurse interrupted. "If you insist so much, I will talk to the Director. Please wait a few minutes." She whispered something to Hino and left.

Mom put her hands on the railing to my bed and sighed.

"I'm sorry for taking so much time."

"That's all right, that's all right. This is going to be a long hospitalization, so you have every right to speak up for the patient."

Hino's refreshing voice dispersed the stale air.

"That's fine, that's fine. We'll check him into room 302 on the third floor."

The big, bearded Director had swept into the room and was talking half to Mom and half to Hino.

Then he looked down at me and said, "You'll have your operation in four days, so for four days you'll have to put up with these weights."

The doctor who had examined me on arrival turned out to be the Director.

"The operation, I want it on Monday!"

I had immediately figured out that four days from now was Monday.

"That's right, Monday. The operation will be on Monday."

The Director left the room, and Mom trotted after him.

As if on cue, Hino and Nakagawa began to move my bed. They returned it to the same position in the same room.

Nakagawa put a needle in my arm, and yellow drops started falling down from a plastic bag above.

It was June 20. For six months, until December 20, this was to be my place. Thinking this, I felt a peace of mind such as I had never known, and then a heavy drowsiness that drew me into a deep sleep.

It was already mid-afternoon when I woke up to a variety of noises. Sunlight flooded through the windows and brightened every corner of the room. I could hear the sound of suppressed giggles next to my ear: "Khhh, khhh, khhh."

"A private room for free? What could be better? You should have taken it!"

With her back to the wall Mrs. Kawabata, Mom's best friend, was sitting in the chair by my bed.

"Be serious. They just couldn't understand that it's not a question of money. There's a limit to how much you can make a fool of somebody. Two thousand yen, and then it's free? Then why don't they give it free to anyone who wants it? Why only Tommy—and then to *request* that he go into a *free* single room!?"

When talking to Mrs. Kawabata, Mom wouldn't mince words.

Using my elbows, I managed to raise a third of my body up. There were four beds in the room. The man in the bed next to mine was reading a newspaper spread out in front of him. The high school boy across the way was sitting up in bed surrounded by three of his friends, all talking loudly. Diagonally across from me, a woman sitting in a chair and the person sitting in the bed had their faces close together. A little girl was running around between the beds, and sometimes running up to them.

"Oh, Tommy's up," said Mrs. Kawabata.

"Tommy, don't you need to pee? From today this bed is going to be your bathroom, you know," said Mom.

Mrs. Kawabata rose. Mom drew a white curtain around my bed and handed me a chamber pot.

"Here, use this. Do a good job!"

Since my babyhood I had been delicate and meticulous about discharging, so in this regard Mom pretty much trusted me.

Despite the weights on my leg, I pulled it off in less than three minutes.

Though it was well past the lunch hour, there in front of me, on the table that bridged the railings of my bed, were a dish of Chinese braised vegetables and meatballs.

"Bravo!" In my heart I raised a silent shout of joy.

So this is hospital life. How easy it is! You just lie in bed. Everything is taken care of. A white curtain separates you from the outside world. Open it and you'll find at least three people out there.

"In your mind there are layer after layer of curtains. Well, maybe three layers. So when I talk to you, I'm always looking for a way to open those curtains. But you only open the outer curtain halfway, and then quickly close it again. You're just impossible! That's why you need help from other people, to force those curtains open."

This is what Mom told me once.

"But it's a whole lot of trouble to try to open somebody's curtain, and people don't want to bother with it, and so for people like you who keep it shut they say, let it stay shut, and we'll collect him along with other people who keep their curtains shut and put them all somewhere together. That's how the world works."

Now I got it. She was talking about this white curtain. So on that point, the hospital makes it easy. Open it, and there's the guy reading his newspaper next to me. So that's it. It must be that the single room that the Head Nurse was pushing has no curtain. Or it may be that there is one, but if you open it there's no one outside.

"Tommy, they look good!" Mrs. Kawabata smiled at me as I stuffed my mouth with the meatballs Mom had reheated in the microwave.

"I wonder how many meters long the new Tanna Tunnel is."

In an attempt to express my absolute happiness, I said one of my hobbyhorse questions. Mom and Mrs. Kawabata exchanged glances. I had only wanted to let them know how good I felt on the first day of my six-month stay in the hospital. But as usual, I missed the mark.

"The new Tanna Tunnel. Now, where was that?"

After a pause, Mrs. Kawabata showed she was thinking about my question, so I was satisfied. I dropped my chopsticks on the table and began humming my favorite melody from Schubert's *Unfinished Symphony*, swinging my upper body.

"Don't, Tommy. You shouldn't move your body," said Mom.

Resigned, I put another meatball in my mouth.

"See, Tommy is always like this. Ahh, maybe I should have taken the Head Nurse's advice after all," Mom grumbled.

"Oh come now, that's not like you. And you decided. I'm sure this will work out best for Tommy."

It went without saying that Mom's whole body was simmering with resolve to hold out in this room no matter what happened. That I knew.

By now all the visitors had left, and except for around my bed the room was silent. The high school boy was reading a comic, and the man diagonally across from me, an office worker who had broken his nose and leg in a traffic accident, was sitting up and writing something at the bed stand. The man next to me, who had had his newspaper spread out before him for an inordinately long time, was maybe only pretending to read it while he sized me up.

Mrs. Kawabata put a bunch of carnations by my bed and left. Mom tidied herself up a bit and stood up by my bed.

"Now, may I introduce your new roommate. His name is Tomio Kashiwagi. He is a little unusual, and he finds it hard to associate with people in an ordinary way, so I'm afraid he's going to cause you some inconvenience, but your indulgence will be appreciated."

By the time the high school boy had raised his head from his comic, Mom's greeting was finished.

"A traffic accident?" asked my neighbor, Makino-san, finally putting down his newspaper.

"Yes. On his way back from his paper route . . ."

Just as Mom began to explain, a middle-aged woman with her body bent double entered the room, quickly looked around, and addressed herself to Mom. "Are you Kashiwagi-san? I've just been told by the police." Her voice betrayed no qualms.

"I am truly sorry. This is the fourth time my son has caused an accident."

"So—you? The police told me they would be able to find out right away who it was."

"He's just a worthless boy. I happened to be on a bus going to the golf club where I work as a caddie. I was idly looking out the window when the bus passed the scene of the accident. My heart stopped because I knew immediately it had to be my son. He'd been out all night, and came back early in the morning. When that boy goes out on his bike, I feel like I'm dead. I got off the bus and went right home, and sure enough, he was there. He had pulled a futon over himself and wouldn't come out. Then, the police came . . ."

Mom suggested several times that they go outside to talk, but the woman paid no attention. Finally she stopped to take a breath, and Mom offered her a chair. You could have heard a pin drop in the room.

"Of course, it's just no good, not having his father with us." The woman muttered and sniffled, her heavy makeup blackening under her eyes.

"My husband left four years ago. Last year he came flitting back for a while, and we got divorced."

"Oh, my. Oh, my."

"But my son has insurance. I know what he's like, so I've gone out of my way to put a voluntary policy on him as well. So the hospital expenses will be covered."

She said this matter-of-factly, as if she had changed into another person.

A policeman opened the door and beckoned with his hand, so Mom and the woman went out. I had the feeling that the woman must be a very nice person.

Four days later they did an operation on my leg that took five hours. I woke to find myself in a dusky room, covered with a plaster cast from my chest down to my left ankle.

Mom's face was right by my side.

"It's all right now, Tommy. Do you hurt anywhere?"

"It doesn't hurt. It doesn't hurt."

My whole body felt torpid. I could see Mom's face, but it seemed vague, as though we were talking through a curtain.

"Today is Monday, June 24. The operation was done on Monday, just as you wished. This is a special room for people who have just had an operation. It's right next to the nurse station."

I stayed in that room for two days. Hino and Nakagawa and the other nurses came to measure my blood pressure, adjust the IV, take my temperature, and what not. On the third day the urination device was taken off and I returned triumphantly to the former room.

My living space had been reserved.

"Welcome back, Tommy. How did it go? My, look at you. You're clad in armor from the chest down."

Makino gave me an affectionate welcome, as if we had known each other for ten years. While I was away, Mom must have spent some time laying groundwork. The other two roommates were all smiles too.

For the four days before the operation, Mom had slept on a folding cot she had put beside my bed. Her greatest concern was to get the other patients, if not to understand my soliloquies and irrelevant questions, at least to tolerate them.

The thing she feared the most was that I might be thrown into that hell called a single room.

"Terrible snores, I won't say who. But compared with that, your monologues are nothing. Actually, they help to offset the boredom."

Mom whispered, but he had sharp ears.

"I'm terribly sorry," said Makino.

"No, no, not at all. Tommy should be." Then she leaned toward him and lowered her voice. "Actually I was hoping that the shock of being knocked in the head might make him a bit more normal," she chuckled. Makino smiled, a bit reluctantly.

Temperature and blood pressure at seven, breakfast at eight followed by the IV, doctor's rounds at ten thirty. This order was absolute, no matter what happened. I was used to getting up at four thirty every morning for my paper route, so the early rising at the hospital was a cinch for me. And of all the patients, I was the most obedient to the hospital routine. If, as happened just occasionally, the IV got delayed for ten minutes, I would push the nurse call button so insistently that the nurses set up "Tommy time" just for our room, under which everything began and ended at exactly the same time each day. Kiriyama-kun, the high school boy, was often off visiting other rooms, and he would have to come rushing back, hobbling on his crutches.

Makino was a high steel worker who had broken his hip falling off a roof. For him as a professional, the shame of the fall mattered more than the injury itself.

"You can't beat old age. That's what my son keeps telling me. He says it's time for me to quit." Whenever the conversation went in that direction, he would become despondent.

In less than a week, instead of me adjusting to them, my roommates adjusted to me, and whenever I asked one of my special questions, one of them would try to answer. When that happened, Mom would look exceptionally happy, and on the very edge of saying, *This is exactly why I insisted on a large room!*

"Somehow I feel comfortable when I come in this room. It's Tommy's doing." When Hino said this, Mom responded,

"It's the two of us, Tommy and me. We are the protagonists of a tragedy, carrying a burden of unheard-of misfortune. I am a widow, over fifty, a woman of no beauty whatever. I have an abnormal son, and now he has a serious injury. We don't know if he will be able to walk again. So anybody who comes in the room and sees us can realize how happy they are, don't you think?"

"I don't know what a tanuki road is."

Mom, Mom, take it easy. Stop feeling sorry for yourself—is what I had wanted to say, but this was all I could come up with. The room fell silent, and then the barber entered from the next room.

"Tommy, it's about time, isn't it?"

Blade in hand, he was coming to give me a shave. In the hospital for a hernia operation, the barber had been giving me a clean shave with his straight razor every three days.

"I . . ." Ishii-san, the white-collar worker in the bed by the window, began talking shyly. With his broken nose it was hard for him to talk.

"I did a bit of research. On that tanuki road thing. I didn't find exactly that, but there's something called 'tanuki digging.' It's a primitive method of mining where you don't design a shaft from the surface, but begin from an outcropping and follow, you know, the natural vein. It also refers to a kind of road construction where you don't use machines, but just dig along little by little with picks and shovels."

He was reading from some notes he was holding.

"So I think a road made in this way could be called a tanuki road."

Ishii had lots of books stacked on a cabinet by the window, and was always reading or writing.

"Tommy-san, don't you think so?"

He startled me with the nonchalant way he asked the question, without expecting an answer.

Ishii had a fixing device attached to his broken nose, with a piece of gauze over it that flapped every time he talked. Seeing that conveyed to me his diligence and warmth, so I was easily persuaded by his interpretation.

"I think that's probably it. Tommy sometimes surprises us with his irony, so—I think that's probably the answer."

The mixed smell of grilled fish and miso soup wafted in from the hall. As was my habit, I looked at my watch. Five minutes early. Well, that was acceptable. My tolerance limit was ten minutes.

The barber left.

We were each served our meals, and just as we started munching the caddie lady came in. Behind her stood a boy with a man-sized body but a junior high school face.

"I am truly sorry. Now, hurry up and apologize."

At the woman's urging, the boy said, "I'm sorry," bowed, and quickly left without looking at my face.

"He's just a worthless boy. This is the fourth time. It's a miracle that the two are still alive. This time I felt I couldn't take it any more, and I tried to reach his father for help, but I couldn't get hold of him. I just don't know what to say, I am so sorry. Of course the insurance will pay the medical bills. . . ."

And she offered a box of sweets to Mom.

"Again, thank you. But maybe, not here—outside?"

Mom pushed her shoulder and the two went out.

Aside from us slurping our soup and munching our food, the room was eerily quiet, but that was just as usual during mealtime. The tension the woman had brought in with her seemed to stagnate the air.

"What a burden to be a parent."

Makino broke the silence in a thoughtful voice. "But they're lucky at least that it was Tommy. My nephew also injured a person badly with his bike, but it was a white collar worker with children, so he had to go through a lot."

As he said this, he glanced at me. But as for me, I was worried every morning about how my paper route was being taken care of.

In my first days in hospital, every night before going to sleep I would ask Mom, "What about tomorrow's papers?"

"This is no time to be worried about such a thing. Really, you choose strange places to put your loyalty." She implied that she was too busy to think about such a small matter.

"I wonder what the departure time of the first westbound bullet train for Hakata is."

What I had really wanted to do was tell Makino that I had a job delivering papers, but somehow it always ends up like this.

"What? How should I know?" said the high schooler.

"I'll look it up," said Ishii consolingly.

This is how things always get off the point, little by little. It's my big trouble. When someone says something about me, and I want to respond, I can never find the words. Then I get impatient, and blurt out something that Mom calls irrelevant. I'd like to communicate the genuine feelings I have deep in my heart, but I still don't have the language to do it. Sometimes I hear people use words that seem pretty close, but then I shake my head, and realize that that is not my *language*.

On the other hand, maybe I just don't understand what my genuine feelings are.

Mom came back, looking tired.

"How did it go?" Makino asked sympathetically. "Looks like the insurance is a big hassle for you too."

"You listen to her stories and you realize she has hardships too, then she and I start feeling sorry for each other and everything gets all tangled up—though the police just call us the wrongdoer and the victim."

Mom quickly cleared away the dishes from my table and picked up the tray.

"Basically I'm just not made for a tearjerker. Two pathetic mother-child pairs holding their handkerchiefs and consoling each other, like one of those old mother-movies. It's enough to give you goose bumps down your spine!"

The other patients were quietly sipping their tea or putting away their chopsticks.

In this way the days passed, and my leg continued healing without much problem. During that time my greatest pleasure was seeing Hino's face. She was the first person I had met when I was brought to the hospital, and after that I would see her every three days. She was two years older than I, and apparently had a child in elementary school.

Several nurses took care of me every day, but she had something the others didn't. There was nothing at all wrong with the others, but when Hino carried out the same tasks they did, there was something delicately different about it. So the best time was when Mom was away, and Hino was on the night shift. I found I needed to go to the bathroom much more often, and again and again my hand would be on the nurse's call button.

"Tommy, aren't you going overboard? You can't really need to go that often," Hino would say as she brought the chamber pot and emptied it.

But the strange thing is that each time I really did have to go, so there was nothing else to do.

"What would happen if my pecker was put in a cast?"

The question just popped up in my mind.

Pfff—stifled laughter came simultaneously from Hino by my side and Makino beyond the curtain. The laughter spread irresistibly to Ishii, who was supposed to be sleeping.

Only Kiriyama snored right through it.

As for me, I was now strangely wide awake, and so I took out my small tape recorder and put the earplugs in my ears. Schubert's *Unfinished* began halfway through the first movement.

Hino was saying something. It was strange to watch her lips moving to the music. She patted the blanket and left.

I made an important discovery. Mom liked the Director just as I liked Hino. It was obvious from the delicate way her expression and manner changed on the days he made his rounds.

Given that it was he who had done the operation and it was he who had permitted me to be in this room, maybe it was inevitable that she would feel totally devoted to him. But to me it didn't look very promising.

Mom was bereaved of Dad when I was five, and ever since had been completely occupied taking care of me. Add to this the fact that it would be hard to call her a beauty either in face or body and you would have to conclude that, while her feelings were understandable, it didn't look like there was much hope.

But still, when the Director came by on his rounds and Mom, eyes dreamy and cheeks flushed, would be unbuttoning my shirt with her grabby hands, their veins and knuckles protruding—at these times I liked her.

And when, with the Director standing beside her, Mom got nervous and couldn't seem to get my pajamas unbuttoned, instead of saying,

"Clumsy!"

I would say,

"I wonder in what year and what month and on what day you will take the cast off."

Because the Director had felt her power at the time the room was decided, and maybe also because he had come to understand me better over time, he was always very gentle to us.

It seems that Mom and I both are of the type that, no matter what adversity we encounter, we manage to find something sweet in it. It's kind of sad.

At the end of July, there is a big fireworks display in our town. A whole lot of fireworks are set off on the bank of the big river.

Although the hospital is rather far from the site, we were told that you can see the fireworks pretty well from the rooftop. Everyone in the hospital had been talking about it from mid-July. We heard that on that night, lights-out would be delayed.

But I was resigned. Impossible with this body.

Every year I used to climb the hill behind our home and watch the fireworks, which seemed so close you wanted to hold out your hands and touch the circles of light. But then I told myself, fireworks are no match for my favorite, the grand sunset. Rather than fireworks or anything else, what I wished for most was to be released from the hospital as soon as possible, and to be standing alone, with no one to bother me, watching the sunset.

On July 28 I had a surprise.

In the evening, when you could see the twilight from the window, Makino, Ishii (who was now able to walk a bit) and Kiriyama on his crutches came over to my bed and began pushing it. They opened the door and wheeled me, still lying down, out of the room.

In the hall they were joined by Hino and Nakagawa.

Up on the rooftop, spread eagle on my bed, I faced the star-filled sky.

Shuru, shuru, shuru—hyuuuuuu, BAAAAN!

The sky showed itself, stark naked.

2

ROMANCE

It looked like the rain was going to pour. I didn't have an umbrella, so I just walked along, letting myself get soaked.

Footsteps and laughter came chasing up from behind me, and then hopped over ahead. A pair of schoolgirls in middy outfits appeared before my eyes.

"Ah ha ha ha! Tommy, what's happened to you? There're soap bubbles floating off your head. Look! Look!"

Kikuchi-san's words were mixed with overflowing laughter, as she pointed to my head. I had been scratching my head from time to time, but it just got itchier, so now I was scratching furiously.

"What's going on? Ah ha ha ha!"

Arashiyama-san dropped her umbrella in the street and dissolved into a fit of laughter.

With my two classmates laughing in front of me, and especially with one of them being that sweet Arashiyama, my body froze and I couldn't move.

We were in the second year of middle school, so that would have been seventeen years ago, while we were coming home from school.

Arashiyama suddenly stood on tiptoe and touched my hair with her hand.

"I've got it, I've got it! Tommy washed his hair. Ah ha ha ha."

"That's it, that's it! Except he didn't rinse it out last night."

"Look. It's the rain on his head and his scratching."

"Take a look at yourself, Tommy."

Kikuchi fought down her laughter, dug out a square mirror from her schoolbag, and stuck it before my eyes. I looked into it, rubbing my head with both hands.

Ah! There really are bubbles!

Amazingly, tiny soap bubbles were soaring up from the top of my head. *Fuwari . . . fuwari . . .*

I rub my head and, look, there's one, and another, and another. Through the now thinning threads of the rain, the crystal spheres rise up toward the sky. And in each one, Arashiyama and I are reflected. Feeling proud I chase after this one, then that one. Peals of laughter echo again.

"OK Tommy, enough is enough. Come under my umbrella." Arashiyama picked up her umbrella, which had landed upside down in the street, and held it over me. "Tommy, you are such fun. . . . See you later."

"Bye. But, Ara-chan, are you okay? Just you and Tommy like that?"

"No problem. He was so funny. To thank him I want to see him home. Bye."

It all happened so fast. Kikuchi went away and I was walking under Arashiyama's umbrella.

"I wonder what day the day after tomorrow will be."

Feeling nervous, I started off with my Question 18, the one about days and dates.

"There you go again. Today is Monday, so it's got to be Wednesday. Stop all that and carry my bag. 'Cause I'm carrying the umbrella."

Arashiyama pressed her school bag into my right hand, which was already holding my own bag. Then she shifted the umbrella to her left hand and slipped her right hand under my arm.

"Look, Tommy, after you wash your hair you have to rinse it over and over, you see, 'til you get all the shampoo out."

Her voice again overflowed with laughter.

Her shoulder-length hair was waving just next to me, and I felt the urge to stroke it and touch my lips to it.

But then I seemed to hear Mom's voice: "*Don't do it! Even though you mean no harm, you are grown up now, and she will be alarmed. If that happens, even I will have to have you locked up somewhere.*"

So I swallowed, and didn't do it. I was able to control myself for the first time ever, I think not so much because I recalled Mom's warning as because I liked Arashiyama so much.

"Hey, that person coming toward us, isn't that your mom?"

Before Arashiyama spoke I had already caught sight of Mom, carrying my umbrella. As she drew near, her look changed from puzzlement to a shy smile.

"Well, thank you. Tomio, lucky you!"

"Oh, don't mention it. Kashiwagi-kun is fun. He was making bubbles with his head. I guess he didn't rinse out the shampoo after he washed his hair. Please have him rinse a little more carefully from now on. Okay, I have to go now. Bye."

She turned to me and waved her hand, and left.

Usually both of them call me "Tommy, Tommy," but today they got all formal, calling me "Tomio" and "Kashiwagi-kun."

I started walking, paying no attention to Mom.

"Which tunnel is the longest tunnel? What happens if you sleep in a tunnel?"

I walked along muttering my stock questions one after another, more to myself than to Mom. When she was talking to Mom, Arashiyama had talked very much like an adult, and that made me feel somehow lonely.

"Well, that was nice. How sweet of her to share her umbrella with you. Here, take this."

I ignored the umbrella that she had brought for me, and began scratching my head again furiously. My rain-wet hair apparently began producing foam again.

Immediately Mom and I were surrounded by lazily floating bubbles.

"Oh my, oh my. What can I do? What can I do?"

Mom forgot about opening the umbrella and began trying to catch the bubbles or brush them away. The people who passed us by looked as though they were both smiling and not smiling. Mom noticed this and quickly came to herself again.

"I can't go into the bath with you any more, so from now on rinse more carefully." Her voice was severe.

"But it was good. Getting you into the same middle school with everyone else was the right thing. Her kindness to you was so natural."

She murmured this as though convincing herself, and raised her umbrella again. Yes, without believing that she can't go on; nobody knows that better than I.

Though I was able to attend a regular elementary school, at the level of middle school it was assumed that a misfit like me would be sent to a special school. In that atmosphere Mom negotiated with the school board and the teachers.

To get me into the school, Mom spoke before a group of about forty teachers. She told them a story about when I was a sixth-grader.

I hated water then. Or rather, I was afraid of it. I had once put my face in the bathwater and tried to breathe. It was awful beyond description. After that I always washed my face in the morning with just my index finger, to keep contact with water to the minimum.

That's why when the time came for the summer swimming class I felt I had been thrown into hell. My teacher was doing everything she could to get me into the water.

I would set up a heart-rending wail and dart around the poolside to run away from her. One of the school's special education teachers saw this and offered to take over my swimming lessons.

When the time for the lesson came the next day, he came to my classroom to pick me up. The moment I saw the burning glow in his eyes, I sensed danger and went wild. But he picked me up and carried me to the special ed classroom, where there were about six other children, some physically weak, some who couldn't walk, some who were always running away. Two woman teachers were helping them get into swimsuits.

I resisted, but he got me into my bathing trunks, and scooped me up into his arms. Then he trotted down to the poolside and, without slowing down his momentum, jumped right into the water.

I had no time to say "Aah" or "Ooh." When I came to myself the bubbles around me had subsided and I saw, over the lucid water, a distant azure sky.

For a moment a strange silence came over me. Still startled, I saw the figures of people swaying on the poolside, and right next to me a pair of beefy legs whose short hair was wafting in the water. I went berserk. I opened my mouth, gulped water, and thrashed my arms and legs.

I was told that from the next day on, in the third period, I was to take daily swimming lessons.

I have an innate adherence to things that are scheduled and to the times they are scheduled, so the struggle between my fear and the absolute sense of obligation to enter the water produced in me severe inner conflict. Every day as the hour approached my heart would be filled with an extraordinarily intense emotion. But maybe you could also say I enjoyed it a bit. And with this conflict whirling inside me, my body steadily learned how to swim. Not that I mastered any stylish form. But by moving my arms and legs I could now get myself from one end to the other of our twenty-five-meter pool.

After a week, the special ed teacher announced triumphantly, "Tommy's ready. Let him swim with the rest of the class from tomorrow."

So he passed the baton to my regular teacher.

I had thought the lessons were over. But the next day I felt like screaming in despair when I realized that the time of the swimming class was again approaching. I prayed that it would come quickly, pass by quickly, and be over quickly.

But then came another big problem. The problem was the way I changed into my swimming trunks. In those days schools didn't have extra rooms, so we would change our clothes in the classroom. The left third was for boys and the right third was for girls, and when the time came friends would help each other to keep out of sight. But I, caring nothing about all that, stripped naked in the middle of the room, and all hell broke loose. Sixth-graders, after all, are already starting to approach adulthood.

"Kyaaa!" "Stop!" "Tommy, don't!"

Girlish voices exploded. But my mind was full with the upcoming swim lesson.

"Goodness gracious! Even though he's a sixth-grader now, not even caring, right in front of everybody. This is real trouble. I will give him a severe talking-to. But may I also ask you, as his teacher, to please do what you can."

Mom shriveled when she heard the story from my teacher. She knew that no matter how severely I was admonished it might not register, and so she could only beg for the teacher's help.

But believe it or not, after a week I was changing with a towel wrapped around my waist. It wasn't because of either the teacher's power or Mom's persuasion. It was the boys in my class, who worked earnestly to teach me to drape myself and avoid the girls' eyes. Maybe they felt ashamed to have a person you wouldn't want to have "upwind from you" as one of their number. But now they truly accepted me as one of their own.

"Maybe they can teach you how to swim in special ed, but they can't teach you manners in changing clothes. To learn that, you have to be in a place where there are lots of people of the same age, so you can teach and learn naturally from each other. Yes, that's a fundamental principle of society, of life. Uh huh, my ideas were proved by Tommy's swimming. It's natural for people to live in a society where all kinds of people are living. And as for learning to swim, you should be able to do it along with everyone else."

Mom started out muttering, but gradually her voice got louder, and finally she quit dusting the bookshelf, tossed the cloth into the air, and began walking around the room.

"I can count this as one specific reason why Tommy should go to middle school with everybody. There are lots of others, but this is *the* reason."

Mom snapped her fingers and resumed cleaning, humming a song.

"I wonder what color and what color and what color a traffic signal is."

I was worried that Mom might be entering into some kind of gigantic cloud, but my question failed to nip her excitement.

"I was really on fire in those days. It's amazing that just one person like me could have that much power inside."

Once a thing was over, Mom would reminisce over and over.

"And as a bonus, since the pool business I have never once seen those important parts of your body. You have mastered the art of using towels as a cover," she laughed.

Oh yes. It was also back then that Mom started campaigning to let students like me attend public high schools. I remember how she collected signatures, moved mayors, school superintendents and the governor, and also lobbied the prefectural board of education.

"Ah! What am I doing? I was going to feed Tommy steak for a change, and here I am breading the beef!"

That's why I've been asking you all along. "I wonder what's for dinner tonight. What's for dinner?" You've been ignoring my important question all the while you were beating the eggs and dusting the flour. Dinner tonight is steak.

Mom was not herself those days. Though seventeen years have passed, I can still call forth images of her in that period, frame by frame, from the storehouse of my memory.

Until then Mom had looked only in my direction or in the same direction as I was looking. But now it felt like she was changing. In the middle of cleaning she would unplug the vacuum and rest on the handle and gaze into the distance.

"I don't know how many tunnels there are on the Sanyo Shinkansen."

Unable to ignore this, I made some attempts with my special technique to bring her to her senses, but nothing worked.

Our phone began to ring more often. Mom was spending more time on the phone and away from home. Watching this, I came to have an unfamiliar unsettled feeling, as if a local train was endlessly thumping and lurching through my chest.

Though even today, when I am over thirty, I still can't make much sense of these things, it might be that Mom had someone who was for her as Arashiyama was for me. I guess that must be it.

I can vaguely understand death in the way that Mom puts it: one day the person stops moving and just disappears. And I can understand that people are born to replace the ones who die, because if they didn't there wouldn't be any people and that would be a problem.

And love?

"Yo, Tommy, Ara-chan is here. Go, go, go! You have a crush on Arashiyama, right?"

My friends would poke fun at me like this, and so I thought, I see, maybe this is what they call love.

I don't know if Mom loved Dad, who died when I was five. But I do know that at that time, when Mom was forty, she was in love. I'm sure of that. And the person wasn't Dad.

"Hey, Tommy. What do you think? Do I look good in this dress?"

Even as Mom was asking me, neither her eyes nor her heart were focused on me. But then she sidled up to me, tousled my hair, gently twisted the buttons on my school jacket and said, "Tonight I'm going to a little get-together, and I might be late. Help yourself to the gratin in the refrigerator. Make sure there's water in the bathtub before you turn on the gas. And also . . ."

She gave me detailed instructions before I left for school, much more meticulous than ever before.

It seemed as though now that she was on the verge of achieving something great, she didn't want any inauspicious incidents coming from me.

There was nothing new in Mom going out a lot, but in the past her instructions had been sketchier, and more dignified. Even when because of me she found her path blocked in all directions, she would always find a way to reorient her stance and look defiantly ahead.

"I wonder what if you put sashimi in gratin." I tried out the question as I was putting on my shoes. The changes in Mom were somehow making me sad.

"There you go again saying something irrelevant. No more of your sarcasm!" That's the way Mom would have lashed back at me before. Then I would have shut the door on her voice and walked out merrily.

"What? Sashimi? Try it, if you think you'll like it."

I blinked. Mom spoke in a strangely silky voice, twirling in front of the mirror by the front door. Mom's gaze was floating in the air, and her heart had flown off somewhere. The railway train began chugging through me again. Not even I would want to eat sashimi in gratin.

Looking up at the clear blue sky I separated from Mom and left for school, to look for a place where I could be for the day.

I was at school all day every day, and so I didn't know everything Mom was doing while I was away, but in those days I sometimes saw Mom writing at her desk.

"I—Tommy will you listen? You can listen in your own way, that's okay; I don't mind if you do your monologue while I talk. I think I have done a lot of things for you. Including things that might never have occurred to me if you were an ordinary kid. But no, I'm so foolishly optimistic, I'd probably be the same with or without you. No, that's not right either. That supposition is unnecessary. The reality is, Tommy is my child and I am his mother. There's no me other than that. But you know, recently I've come to see something very clearly. All the things I've done for you, I've done for myself. It's true. That's the way human beings are. Hey, Tommy, don't you think so?"

She brought out the bottle of beer that she had half emptied at dinner.

"Have some, Tommy. It's okay, it's okay." She brought two tumblers too.

Amber liquid flowed into the glasses as if it had nowhere else to go. You wouldn't call it beer.

Mom sometimes has me drink beer, and I don't dislike it, but tonight it was far from tempting. At the same time it seemed to me that it would be unwise policy to go against her just then, so I poured it down my throat.

"Now that you are in the second year of middle school, you can't keep on clinging to your mother. I say that, but actually it's I who've been doing the clinging. I'm beginning to understand that I'm the one who has to become independent—from Tommy."

"I wonder what the first lesson will be tomorrow."

Mom was acting a little different from usual. I tried lobbing one of my regular questions.

"Since you have zero possibility of going to college, you will have to become independent sooner than your friends. That will be the hardest of all. So that wherever you go, wherever you hang out, at least nobody will come accusing you and there will always be strangers to help you when you need it—not your Mom, but complete strangers. They might be neighbors, they might be people riding on the same train with you. And it's better if I'm not there. That's what I've long believed, and it's true, if you want the people around you to behave like that. If you don't change yourself first, other people will never change. It's not Tommy, it's I who have to become independent."

Mom rhapsodized, brandishing her pen and pointing it at me, but maybe because of the bad aftertaste of the beer, I remained lukewarm. Anyway neither she nor I was about to become independent so easily.

While she's saying this and that, maybe she has just become weary of living with me. But wait, weariness is not what I feel from her now. Rather she seems to be on a high, drunk on her own words.

Anyway, she was changing from the way she was before. Before she controlled my every move, nagging and regulating. Now she was suddenly taking off both hands and trying to cut me loose.

The local train rushed all through my body, and from my mouth gushed an endless monologue.

"Aaaaaaaah! That's the way you are. Here I am trying to talk to you seriously. Well, that's all right. From now on when you go on like that, I'll just ignore you. That's what it means to be independent. For both of us."

Aaaaaaaah, I was beginning to get tired of it myself. Sleepy too. Maybe the local train wanted to return to its station.

I made a big yawn and went upstairs.

One day about three months later I found several sheets of writing paper scattered around Mom's desk. I'm not good at reading, but I thought of copying them out. I'm able to duplicate Chinese characters that I can't read and passages that I can't understand, so that's what I decided to do. Maybe on these pages there's something about this independence that Mom's been talking about. Maybe there's something hidden in there that could explain that train that keeps running through my body more and more often.

Luckily Mom wasn't home that day, so I sat at the desk for the first time in my life and began to make a duplicate on the blank sheets that had been left there.

Monday, January 11, 1969. Rainy. University of Tokyo student movement intensifies. Violent clashes between the Yoyogi and anti-Yoyogi forces. January 18. Sanctioned by the university's Acting President Kato, riot police stormed Yasuda Hall to remove the barricaded anti-JCP Socialist Student Alliance students, to no avail. Students from Nihon University, University of Tokyo and other anti-JCP groups demonstrated near Ochanomizu station. They clashed with the police. Railway service disrupted for a while on the Chuo line. January 19. Students removed from the Hall. Four hundred or more arrests.

I wrote this in my diary one day in November the year before last. A simple diary. Merely a collection of items learned through television and newspapers. Indeed, this year as well as last, the society I live in has developed against the backdrop of the extension of those events.

Still, nothing is different from yesterday around me. After my son goes to school, I clear the breakfast table, clean the house, and plan dinner. Meanwhile I may think about Okinawa, or I may not, either way is okay.

This lackadaisical frame of mind forms a tumor in a corner of my brain. The lump may disappear someday if I keep it just as it is. Thus I have peace around me, at least for now.

But that tumor may sooner or later turn into an obstinate cancer called inertia, and secrete pus that will force its way all through my body. And I may not recognize the pus as pus, but live out my life wearing a faint smile, with excuses and hypocrisy trailing along behind me.

Today, however, the scalpel cut all too well. My usual daily routine failed to keep the tumor in check. All morning I remained upset as I went about my grocery shopping and housecleaning.

What eventually got me out of the house and propelled me into the demonstration was a telephone call from Tajima. As usual I asked for his advice on personal matters—mostly about my son at school—before moving on to the subject that was weighing on me: Okinawa.

Tajima was calling from his office, and it seemed he couldn't talk in depth.

After giving me some helpful suggestions as usual, he casually asked, "Why don't you come to the rally at Ogi-cho Park?"

"Is it all right for someone like me?"

The moment I asked it, I realized with a shock what a stupid question that was. The question was not whether I was allowed to go, but whether I would. The kind of self-hatred that I always feel after talking to Tajima hit me early this time, and my body grew hot.

"Of course it's okay. We'll be going at five."

"All right. I'll think about it, and come if I can."

Having said that, I still had a bunch of nitpicking doubts dangling before my nose. I put down the phone, pushed aside that train of thought, and set my mind to go.

Then all at once I was busy. Got to prepare my son's dinner and his bath. Got to leave by four in order to reach the meeting place by five. I was careful to arrange things so as to keep the constants in his routine, so that everything would proceed as usual, except that I would be absent. Today especially I don't want any trouble from my son, who is so terribly particular and prone to panic.

While I was thinking these things, my bouncing heart rendered me nimble in the kitchen.

Since I first met Tajima in a circle of friends a couple of years ago, I have often felt inspired by him and swayed by his words. We meet every now and then or talk on the phone, and the things we talk about go straight to my heart, and make me think. Though I am aware of this in me, why do I avoid confronting it?

I stood in front of the mirror in my white blouse and blue jeans, selected after much vacillation my most modest navy blazer, and left home. After hearing Tajima's words I had set aside all my doubts, and walked. I loved myself for that, and wanted to cherish that feeling.

But at the station, seeing all the different groups under their red and blue banners, I hesitated. I wondered whether, rather than joining the demonstration, I might end up as a bystander.

No, not today. Today I want to throw myself into the crowd. If not, then tomorrow I'll be sitting at home nursing a tumor even more malignant than the one I've had up to now.

Tajima had said, "We go at five," but now I was regretting hanging up the phone without asking him if five meant the time they would leave the office, or the time they would arrive here. I was also a bit disgusted with myself for deciding to come on the careless assumption that it would of course be easy to find his group in the midst of this confusion.

But then in the next moment I decided it would be okay for me to be alone. Also okay to be a bystander. If I came all this way and discovered after all that I was no more than a bystander, a rubberneck, that would give me something worth thinking about. On the other hand even if I joined the demonstration, I might still keep the psychology of an onlooker.

Anyway I'll go as far as the park. There I will either be—
A person who joined the demonstration,
A person who watched from the sidelines,
A person who ran away—
I followed the tide of people to the park.

It was after five. The last rays of the sunset glowed in the west of the autumn sky, the chill, dark colors enveloping the passion, determination, anger, and excitement of the people on the ground.

The sight of the riot police lined up outside the park hit me like a wave dashing against a cliff.

I had only seen them on television, wearing their masks and holding their shields. Now here they were next to me, pressing down, and clearly not on my side.

I wondered what kind of emotional swings might be hidden under their blue uniforms. Tomorrow morning when they wake up, I suppose that each one of them will be in a room, and in a *futon*, no different from those of any of the other young people who had come to the rally. Although their domestic lives were about the same, because of a difference in their means of supporting themselves, they had to come here for a confrontation.

Looking at the expressionless array of shields, I thought that these people ought to be on the same side as us, and it made me feel sad about human beings.

I had copied this far when the phone rang. It rang eight times without stopping, so I put down my pencil and picked up the receiver.

For some reason I hate odd numbers of anything. Buns or tangerines, I don't feel comfortable unless there are at least two. I also eat in even numbers. If there are three or five sparrows perched on a power line, I feel queasy. I'm past thirty, but it's still the same.

"Maybe you have two hearts, Tommy. Yes, that must be it. That's why you can live so audaciously. No concern for the feelings of others," Mom once grumbled.

"Hello—"

I heard a voice, then it stopped. It was a male voice that I'd never heard before.

"I wonder who it is," I ventured.

"Ah, it's Tommy-kun, isn't it?"

The voice sounded pumped up with energy. "You're doing so well, aren't you? I've heard a lot about you from your mother, I feel like I've known you for a long time—I wonder why."

My upbeat mood for having successfully picked up the phone at the even number of eight rings was for some reason shattered.

"I wonder if Mom's coming home. I wonder what time."

I said just that, and hung up.

I picked up the pencil again. For me, just copying is not so unpleasant.

In the dark square, the black crowd of people and their hubbub form a whirlpool. Voices howling through microphones sucked in and muddied the air, and made it hard to breathe. The stars just appearing in the sky above were irrelevantly white, and I felt an unbearable pang of solitude.

"Down with the Sato administration!"

The cry came from nearby, and set me in motion to look for that labor union.

I approached a number of the flags waving here and there to make out the names on them. Wandering to and fro, I asked several people, but they all seemed to be too occupied with their own thoughts. Which at last forced me to think how really I should spend this evening.

I thought, I could just go home now. Or, I could demonstrate with a group of people I don't know. But still I wanted to give it a last try to see if Tajima was there.

Yes, I had to look for him.

I spoke to a young man perched on an iron fence at the end of the park.

"The Journalists' Union? Oh, they've left the demonstration already. But I think they'll be coming back here again."

"I see. Thank you."

I sat down beside him, feeling tired as if I had walked a long way.

Inside his jacket and jeans there was the smell of youth.

"I'm waiting for a group from my university too," he added. "I had things to do, and left the campus early."

His eyes contained the question, "What on earth are you doing here?" but at the same time, because we shared a purpose, they were friendly.

"Ahh, I don't belong to any organization. I came because I couldn't sit still after I learned about this issue on television. But if I can't find the Union, I don't know what I should do."

I hunched my shoulders and put my worries frankly into words.

He seemed surprised, and gazed at me for a moment.

"My name is Sata. I'm in the graduate school in the department of science and technology at Shiroyama University. Glad to meet you."

"My name is Kashiwagi. When I think about my child's school, and about the problems of education, I realize there are contradictions in society, and that there are things I need to learn, even little by little. And it seems unfair that it's students like you who have to bear the brunt in all kinds of struggles."

"That's how it has to be. We have maybe a little more time to think, and a little bit of power."

In his words, I felt an unassuming delicacy.

"During the campus struggles I was nonsect, and I still am, but then I was close to being nonpolitical, which is now painful to think about."

"Haaa."

"Since then the pressure has increased, and a lot of students have sold out, but there are others who are holding on. Anyway you can't get a good job with an arrest record. My father used to work for the police, so he's always after me."

I tried to imagine the circumstances of his life. His face, coming out of a daily life so different from mine, was something new to me.

The amplified voices phased out, and the people coming and going, rushing around with cameras and passing out leaflets all went out of view. All I had before me was Sata's face and voice.

"I don't totally deny organization. I suppose they are sometimes necessary and it's natural for people to form them. Even so I want to make choices using my own eyes, my own ears, and my own mind. I want to help an organization as long as I agree with it."

His long hair hung over the boyish nape of his neck, and his eyes, peering at me through the darkness, sometimes flashed.

Hmmmmmmm. Here I threw down the pencil, fell flat on my back, and stretched my arms and legs spread-eagle.

Mom has a world that I don't know. She has gotten to know somebody who I don't know, while I wasn't there. I don't understand the details, but by copying Mom's writing I can get the general idea. I wonder what Tajima is like?

"The kind of self-hatred that I always feel after talking to Tajima hit me early this time, and my body grew hot."

Suddenly this sentence leaped from out of the manuscript and hit me square in the heart. The local train in my chest jerked back into motion.

I see. The man on the phone must have been Tajima. I wanted to do anything to quiet that rattling and clattering in my chest. So I went back to the desk.

Sata rose abruptly, said "I think I'll look for my friends," and left.

A sudden wind wailed around my feet. A stranger offered a leaflet to me. Voices through microphones cracked against the night sky.

In the last few days, news about the railroading of the bill for the reversion of Okinawa had passed through my eyes and ears and shaken my heart. I don't know much about the political background. But if the islands are returned with U.S. military bases and nuclear weapons intact, doesn't that mean that the Okinawans, who are just like us, are going to be victimized yet again? Hasn't Japan's postwar prosperity been built on their lives under oppression?

But these were no more than ideas floating around in my head.

Okinawa as an abstraction always flits away from me. In the space vacated by its disappearance, sloth, hypocrisy, and excuses sit cross-legged. And my thoughts, which I am unable to capture as my own, turn into impatience and frustration, forming a tumor in the corner of my brain.

And it was Tajima's phone call that set me in motion.

I turned up the collar of my coat and stood up. Above the tumult, I could hear the sound of my sigh.

A black figure emerged from the darkness and, with bashful friendliness, stood beside me again.

"It seems my friends haven't arrived. I didn't see the Union either."

"Thank you so much. But I have given it up."

I dropped my shoulders.

"Why don't you walk with us? You'll be absolutely safe if you stay right in the middle. Let's do it together."

"Oh, may I?"

My voice danced. *Anyway why not walk? Why not do what I can?*

In the swirling heat, I spotted a flag on which was written, "Student Union, Science and Technology Department, Shiroyama University."

"Hey, guys!"

Sata casually raised his hand in greeting. The students looked at me with smiles on their lips and questions in their eyes.

"Your sister?" someone asked.

"This lady came by herself. She can't find a group she can join. She can walk with us, okay?"

"I'd be happy if you'd let me." I bowed politely.

"By all means, join us! Hurray!" The tightly packed group swayed back and forth. A man with a whistle dangling from his neck and a mike in his hand came up next to me and said in a low voice, "Let's give it our best!" Something banged against my chest, and penetrated inside.

Sata brought another young man over to me, and introduced him to me.

"He's from Okinawa."

Here before me was a person who could identify with today's demonstration with every fiber of his body. I felt heat rising in my throat.

"Let's give it our best," I found myself saying.

I was told that students from all the departments of the university had gathered, and their representatives would address the crowd.

I sat down on a leaflet Sata laid on the ground for me. Before me, behind me, and on both sides of me young people sat packed together. There was no escaping now; I was one of them.

The delegates took turns at the mike, appealing to the crowd.

"Down with the Sato administration!" "No to the Okinawa Treaty!" "Block ratification!" "Smash the Fourth Defense Plan!" "Impeach Professor XX!" Their voices quavered.

To every slogan, the audience responded "Right on!" or "Nonsense!" in unison.

"Maybe you can't hear them very well. They're all saying about the same thing." Sata sometimes turned toward me to explain, followed by a big shout of "Right on!" When his body touched my shoulder through his jacket, a tremor ran through me.

Our group began to move in tight formation, arm in arm, with our hands pressed against the backs of the students in front of us.

Their ideas kindled fire inside their bodies, and the battle began. On my left was Sata, on my right, a tall, spindly boy. Beyond them there was one more student on each side; I was immersed in the smell of young men's bodies.

Silver shields formed a wall, along which a current of dry air flowed. It was all I could do to keep my arms locked together with the boys beside me; my hands couldn't reach the person in front. Sata's big hand moved, glistening, right beside me. For a fleeting second, I wanted to touch it.

We moved forward, our shoes hitting the pavement, *za! za! za!*

When the leader blew his whistle and yelled "Treaty!" we all shouted "No!"

When he yelled "Ratification!" we shouted "Block it!" The voices spread over the ground and echoed back.

Against my will, my words would die at the back of my throat. But my body became accustomed to the motion, swaying from left to right without resistance.

Sata looked into my face to urge me on: "No!" "Block it!"

Beads of sweat flew from his forehead.

"No!" "Block it!"

My voice rose from pianissimo to forte.

"Hurray!"

I wanted to cry out.

Sata smiled at the corners of his lips.

"Let's go to the planetarium."

It was Mom's idea. Maybe a week had passed since I copied her manuscript. It was Sunday.

"I want to see those starry skies. It's been so long." Saying this, Mom came into my room. Then her eyes fell on the words I had written.

"Eh! Did you copy this? Really? Aaah! I don't believe this."

In the middle of Mom's crimson face, her mouth gaped wide.

"But, but I'm sure you don't understand what it's about, do you?"

She looked like she was about to bite me.

"Ahhhhh, no, that couldn't be. What I feel like doing now is shouting 'Idiot! How dare you read my writing in secret!' and starting a big fight with you, Tommy."

Perhaps to avoid sinking into melancholy, Mom poked my forehead a bit.

"Anyway, I felt so happy the other day, when you came home with a face that showed that someone had punched you proper. That was the first time anyone really hit you, wasn't it?"

It was. I was thunderstruck.

"Tommy, the next class is manual training. We move to the room on the second floor." Nakahara-kun, who was generally kind enough to talk to me like this, one day suddenly punched me with his fist.

That one punch was in dead earnest. It was full force. It hurt. Whenever I remember it, my chest and cheeks tighten, and a strange warmth spreads through my body.

In those days, middle school bathrooms for students were large, dark, and uninviting.

On the other hand, the teachers' bathrooms were small, bright, and clean. As if it were perfectly natural, I used the teachers' bathrooms. My classmates found out about this, and apparently talked it over and decided that they should work together to correct my wayward behavior.

After that, whenever it looked like I was heading for a bathroom, someone would say something like, "Tommy, you aren't going to the teachers' bathroom, are you?" or "Tommy, you do understand, don't you?" Sometimes a gang of them would troop along behind me all the way there.

But I still wanted to use the teachers' bathroom. For some reason, the more my friends argued against it, and the more I understood that I shouldn't do it, the greater was the tendency of my body to swerve in that direction.

Among my classmates, the class chairman Nakahara was especially serious and energetic. Every morning, with a sour face, he'd preach to me: "Rules are important, Tommy, at school or anywhere. Sometimes we don't like them either: Don't do this, don't do that, do this, do that. But that's the way it is. You just have to put up with it— you, too, Tommy. You have to grow up too, you know."

To tell the truth, I didn't know if I liked him or not.

Students with good grades generally treated a person like me as though I didn't exist, but Nakahara was different. In the 1,200-meter run and in the marathon, he always ran with me, and would cheer me on enthusiastically.

In spite of that, or rather because of it, I would get a bit self-conscious when he came up to me, and would stave him off with something like, "I wonder what class Nakahara-kun will be in next year."

It happened on one of those days, a Thursday. Thinking that no one was looking, I was making a dash for the teachers' bathroom, when Nakahara spotted me.

"Tommy, wait! Tommy!"

He cornered me at the end of a hallway and, his face scarlet and twitching, hit me hard in the face.

Mom was aghast to see me come home with a swollen chin and cut lip, but then my teacher called from the school and she got the story in perspective.

"Hmmm. Lucky you, lucky you. I'm delighted. To be hit by your friend. I like Nakahara-kun. He really thinks of you as a friend." Mom's voice broke, and she started to cry.

But what I remember more clearly than the rest is that the next day Nakahara, his face all wrinkled up in a smile, patted me two or three times on the back. With that, it felt like what was in his mind came streaming into my body, and from that time on, every time my feet seemed to be heading for the teachers' bathroom, something in my heart would stop me. But it wasn't until the Thursday after the following Thursday that the wounds on my lips and chin were healed.

"Well, anyway it's nice that you're so good at copying words. So, yes, why don't you do something like Soseki's *Cat*, or a piece by Oe Kenzaburo next time. I'll leave the books out."

What! What! Stop right there! Give me a break. I just did it because I wondered what Mom had written. No, I won't be set up.

"I wonder what's for dinner tonight." I tried out this response.

"Come on, Tommy, let's go to the planetarium. It's a wonderful place. It's just made for you. After lunch, okay?"

So Mom ignored me, and returned to the previous topic. I had been to the planetarium several times. I loved it there. I had visited there on school outings and also by myself. But for Mom to invite me . . . ?

My mind filled with a vision of a ceiling overhead transformed into a wide starry sky, music sometimes loud and sometimes soft, commentary like TV news. Unusually for me I said, "I'll go to the planetarium."

"Ahhh, that's good." Despite her words of relief, Mom couldn't calm down.

She put a few croquettes she had bought on a dish. "This is lunch, okay? We've got to leave by one o'clock."

She just put the dish on the table as is, and sat down.

"Oh, yes!" She bounced up again, opened the refrigerator. She peeled two or three leaves from a cabbage, shredded them, and set them before me.

"And then there was broccoli, oh, here it is." She jumped up again, and put the broccoli in the microwave.

Back in her chair, she bit into her croquette.

"Forgot the rice!"

But the rice had already been served. I did it.

"I wonder if it will be the northern hemisphere or the southern hemisphere today."

I said this trying to calm her. That was about the planetarium. But Mom's mind seemed to be somewhere else. With a blank face she munched on her rice and croquette. When the microwave beeped, she didn't notice. I pretended not to hear it, because I don't like broccoli.

Then came a big fuss. As far as I observed she changed clothes four times, putting on and taking off, taking off and putting on. And each time she would pose before the mirror. Once in a while, maybe because she caught a glimpse of me from the corner of her eye, she would wince, but only for a fleeting instant.

When I finally left the house with her, Mom was dressed in a yolk-yellow sweater and a brown check skirt.

Outside, the sky was a light overcast. On an otherwise nonde-script afternoon, only the air around Mom was shimmering. Not wanting to get involved, I walked at a distance from her. But even so she drew near me several times to say, "Don't do too much monologue, okay? Because we're meeting someone today."

We arrived a full hour before the three o'clock opening time. Maybe because it was Sunday, eleven people were already queued up at the entrance. An odd number right at the beginning. Today isn't my lucky day.

Contrary to my expectations, Mom didn't meet anyone special at the gate.

Once we got inside the dome, it was my world. I tilted my reclining chair all the way back, closed my eyes, and imagined the starry skies that were about to appear.

Then I heard Mom's voice in a pitch higher than usual. I looked and saw a man taking the seat next to her. Apparently she had saved it for him.

When the man saw that my eyes were open he began to move, but the opening music had already begun and we were engulfed by the sky of a spring evening.

The sun set and the stars came out across the whole sky. Strauss's *Tales from the Vienna Woods* was playing, sometimes loudly and sometimes softly, while the commentary went on.

On a usual day, by now I would be Pegasus. I would have soared up into the dome, right to the center of the Andromeda Nebula. But not today. Mom and that man were dangling from the tips of Pegasus's wings. No way could I happily ride the wind.

It's Tajima. The guy who was in Mom's manuscript is now holding her hand and clutching my wing.

Look, there's Cassiopeia! There's Orion! And next is Centaurus! I tried to pick up speed among the stars, but they wouldn't let go. They swung this way and that, but kept hanging on.

Outside, it was windy. Tajima, who was tall, walked ahead, with Mom behind and me at her heels.

The three of us sat around a table at a Chinese restaurant. Mom alternated between exaggerating my virtues and exaggerating how difficult I was.

Outside again, the stars were just coming out. They stood side by side and looked at me.

"I'll see you later, Tommy. You go home first. I think I'll be back around ten."

Mom's face was melting into the dusk.

"We'll meet again. Keep it up, Tommy-san." Tajima bent forward to say this to me.

I said, "I wonder if the planetarium will be open tomorrow too."

"Don't forget to turn off the gas after your bath." Mom came over to whisper this in my ear, and then they both turned their backs on me.

That was way back seventeen years ago.

Arashiyama-san has become the mother of two. Mom told me so when she was reading this year's New Year greeting cards.

3

BLACAMAN BEGINS

The Blacaman troupe began on a windy day in spring when Tōta-san visited my house on his motorcycle.

Every morning I get up at half-past four and deliver newspapers to homes in the Larkhill district where I live. I have the kind of character that, when there's something that has to be done I get caught up in it, and until it's finished I can't go on to something else. That's why this job, which I can finish in about an hour in the early morning, is just right for me.

I love it that when I put the papers in the proper mailboxes at the proper times, the number of papers is sure to decrease, and it's a wonderful feeling to pedal home through the sunrise with just the two extra papers left in the basket on the rear of my bike. Once in a while, when because of some glitch in my head I end up riding home with three papers, or maybe none, I feel unbearably irritated. All the pent-up troubles and grievances of daily life seem to flood through my body, and I ride home blathering to myself in a loud voice.

When that happens I know Mom will scold me again, but once my monologue begins like this there's no one in the world who can stop it.

Naturally I'm proud of my job, but Mom is not. Yesterday two of her friends came to visit, and when I joined them Mom said, as if to smooth things over, "Tommy does a paper route. It's good for his health too."

Wanting to make a mild protest I said, "I'll prepare the bath today."
I tried to read her face.

"That will be good. Yesterday we only took showers." Mom turned
toward me and answered in a low voice, before she quickly returned
her gaze to her friends who, not knowing what else to do, exchanged
smiles.

My real intention had been to ask her to show a little more re-
spect for my newspaper delivery job, but when the intention took
the form of words it came out entirely different: "I'll prepare the
bath today." That's my bad habit, or maybe my strangeness. Mom
never gets my true message. Or maybe she doesn't want to get it. Or
she gets it but pretends not to. In this way our feelings for the last
thirty years have been like a pair of rails on a railroad track that
never come together.

Anyway, Tōta came that day after I had finished my morning routine, had climbed back into bed and was melting into sleep. The
pitter-patter of Mom's slippered feet down the hallway to answer the
door told how upbeat she was.

"Tommy, come down. Tōta-san is here."

I heard her call me from the bottom of the stairs. I was wide
awake but did not feel like going down. She would definitely set the
pace in everything, so things wouldn't be so different even if I stayed
in bed. I placed a record on the turntable and flipped the switch.
Schubert's *Unfinished Symphony* began as usual. It's a vinyl that was
bought when I was three, so it's more than thirty years old. Mom is
not happy about this, saying nobody uses such an old stereo player
today, but I love this vintage thing.

By the way the name I go by, Tommy, Mom also gave me at that
time. My paternal grandfather, I am told, had insisted on naming me
Tomio, which included one of the Chinese characters from his
name, Toshio. Mom objected because it sounded archaic, but Dad,
who is dead now, agreed and she was steamrollered. Perhaps to re-
coup her loss, when I grew old enough to understand things—
though I certainly didn't understand things in the ordinary way—
she gave me this nickname that sounds like an American's. So I am
still Tommy though I'm past thirty.

This antique disc is scratched so badly that the stylus skips and hops. Sometimes I have to lend a hand to play the music. I feel sorry for the Berlin Philharmonic. For myself, I don't mind if andante is changed to allegro. After all, this is my good old *Unfinished*.

As I was listening, prodding the stylus into the grooves with my fingertip, Tōta called from downstairs. "Tommy-san, won't you come down? Can we have a talk?"

It would be rude to ignore him, so I stopped the music and went down to the living room.

Tōta is twenty-four years old. He still goes to university. I have a weakness for people who are younger than I am. That's because it's not in my nature to think much about the future. Rather I have precise recollections of thousands of incidents from my childhood and teenage years stored in the corners of my brain, and I retrieve a few of them each day and superimpose them on the present, relishing them like a baby does its pacifier. That's maybe why I'm so interested in how a younger person is going through that period of their life, in comparison with how it was for me when I was that age. In particular I am curious about what is in the minds of the little ones. When I meet children on the street I feel as if I have to ask them in person, but end up being restrained by the people around me when I try to get close.

I had hardly sat down when Mom said cheerfully,

"A drama troupe. Let's start a drama troupe."

"Hmmmm . . ."

Tōta let out a low moan, blinking his eyes and giving the impression of deep thoughtfulness.

"Well, that's an idea, but I wonder if a puppet theater might not give more opportunities to people like Tommy."

It would have been better to be more straightforward, but he was diffident and vague.

"I hate to take exception to you who are always so nice to Tommy, but I have a problem with that kind of thinking. Deciding that certain things are right for certain kinds of people. I want to think just the other way around."

"Easy, Mom, easy," I was murmuring in my heart.

"I wonder what day of the week Friday last week was."

The question popped out of nowhere.

With a there-you-go-again expression, Mom sighed and looked at me.

"Friday last week was Friday."

Tōta came up with just the response I expected. That question is one of my favorites, and always ranks high in my verbal repertoire.

Mom calmed down some and her eyes softened a bit as she gazed at him.

"What I want to say is, I don't want to follow conventional wisdom; I want to go against it. A play is language. There's a script. It's about human relationships. I want to focus on the things Tommy and the others are weakest at. If you think about it that way, a drama troupe is just the thing."

Looking at Mom, Tōta's eyes brightened. "Definitely. Point well taken. In a theater there are plenty of jobs like props and sets. It should be a lot more fun."

Mom flashed dissatisfaction at his comment. I could read her mind. Why is it difficult for us to become actors, but okay to become stagehands? She didn't like that bias in his words. But I could also understand his way of thinking.

"In theater, the action is big in scale, and in a sense it's a world of make-believe, so it can be done." Mom's voice softened as she sensed that Tōta had moved closer to her side. "Rehearsal twice a month. We can meet at the new civic center."

He was now totally in.

"But I wonder if they can really do it?" Suddenly all the confidence drained out of Mom's voice. This always happens with her. When things start to move in the direction she wants, she starts to get anxious.

"They'll do fine. We have been worrying about how to get on with Tommy and the others from now on, and this is what we came up with." Now it was Tōta who was unruffled.

It was four years before that I, Yōko-san, Takeshi-san, and Yōji-san joined Tōta-san's college group. We started visiting his campus once a week. The harmonica club he belonged to took us in, and we would eat together and go on picnics. Tōta was the central figure, and would mediate between us and the other students, and take care of things like negotiating with the administration so we could enter the clubroom on the campus.

Generally when I try to communicate to someone what is in my mind, I tend to be timid and guarded. When I have something deep in my heart that I want someone to understand, paradoxically this blocks me from getting the words out. Or when I am occasionally able to speak honestly, for some reason we fail to connect, and the other person gets angry or gives me a lecture. Even Mom and I talk past each other, after all these years. This is a difficult problem.

Tōta is set to graduate in March. It seems he has been thinking about how to relate to us in the future, and has had many discussions with Mom. She had been counting on his prediction last fall that he might be unable to graduate because he was failing French, but now he seems to be ready for commencement. Mom's plans for another year of weekly visits to the campus were shattered, and she is scrambling for a new plan.

"We don't want this to be like a student recital."

Tōta's words drew a deep nod from Mom.

"'These kind of people are in the play; please come and watch them.' That would be awful."

They were talking about me, but they exchanged nods forgetting that the central figure was right by their side. Once this thing starts it is sure to be followed by, "Come on, you can do it! You can do that much!"—Mom's pep talk.

I took a sip of tea indifferently.

"Tommy-san, what about a drama troupe? I think it would be fun." Tōta looked into my face.

"I wonder what a drama troupe is. I wonder if Tōta-san lives in a condo or in a regular house."

Out came the kind of question I am so good at. I wanted to express my many feelings to Tōta, who had been thinking so earnestly.

"I live in a condo."

Tōta casually answered my question, which I had put to him countless times since we met, while Mom flashed a reproachful look my way. Her eyes were a bit milder than they would have been if we had been alone, but that was for show. Probably as much frustration was building up inside her.

The drama troupe was launched. It was made up of Tōta and two of his university friends, plus me, Yōko, Takeshi, and Yōji, each joined by our respective mothers. The troupe was named *Blacaman*. Tōta borrowed the name from the title of a short story written by the Latin American author Gabriel García Márquez, *Blacaman the Good, Vendor of Miracles*.

Tōta was the troupe leader. Mom boosted me into the position of deputy troupe leader. Of course that meant Mom and me working in tandem, as in a three-legged race. Her feeling was that unless at least in name I got put out in front, the four of us who weren't good at expressing ourselves would be pushed into the background and we would lose track of why the troupe had been founded in the first place. She explained this frankly before everyone, and I got the job.

One day a boy named Saburo joined the troupe. Yōji had met him on the train returning from the campus.

Yōji had spotted a small opening between two passengers and tried to wriggle in his hips to take a seat. One of the passengers, a gentleman who had been dozing, tried to push him away with an irritated look. But Yōji is not one to be deterred by something like that. The man got seriously upset. The car was in an uproar.

Saburo, who was sitting in the seat directly opposite, quietly got to his feet and let Yōji sit in his place. The gentleman's red face returned to normal, and things quieted down. But Saburo worried about Yōji getting off the train by himself, and so walked with him all the way to his home, with the result that he ended up joining the drama troupe.

There was a bonus. A pretty student from a women's college, Mio-san, who happened to be in the same car saw the whole thing, was impressed by Saburo's act, and followed them. In the end she also joined the troupe, and she and Saburo became a loving couple.

It's a mystery how people's paths cross. In the hope of crossing more paths, we decided to put up a recruiting poster.

Tōta, for some reason, drew a large picture of a human face that looked like a horse, and below that Mom wrote,

"Regardless of gender, age, or nationality, do you want to become someone entirely different from your present self? Would you like to take care of costumes, lighting, or music in a theater? Would you like to manage the whole thing? Everyone is welcome."

It seems it's always exciting when something new begins. In the middle of cooking and cleaning, Mom would suddenly let her arms drop and fall into thought. When that happened she didn't seem to notice me even if I sneaked up on her.

But as for me, as I said before, I am so fainthearted that when I encounter a new thing or a first experience, I first of all withdraw into my shell and close the door tight.

Apparently Mom can't bear it if she can't pull me into her game, so she uses all her power to envelop my body and soul. In the present world—I know this sounds overblown—the result of a contest between me and Mom is as clear as fire is bright. So I resign myself, but then there are times that I can't help hurling every one of my available questions at her.

Then Mom gets mad and says, "That's not what we're talking about now. Don't say irrelevant things." But as for me, I think these pop-up questions are strongly related to the true feelings buried deep inside me. For her part, Mom has a veteran's confidence based on the long years she has been with me, and quickly brings me back to her pace.

"Tommy, we are going to rehearse the play twice a month. With Tōta-san and the others."

Feeling the signs of one of her pep talks coming, I blurt out,

"I don't know when you will die."

"There you go again, calling yourself 'you.' You mean to say 'I' don't you?"

Oh, right. I should have said, "I don't know when I will die." I'm too modest about talking about myself so that instead of "I," I tend to use the name that others call me: "you." Mom is accustomed to this, and just corrects my mistake without a trace of surprise.

"Tommy, do you remember? You were in the fifth grade. The school play was called—what was it—yes, *Somewhere on the Planet*. You were the sun, and you held up a sun made of cardboard and walked from one side of the stage to the other. It was in the school gym, remember?"

Of course I remember. No one can match me in the accuracy with which I keep the memories of my childhood. They are what support my present. I'm not much good at imagining the future, but by linking my present self to the past, I create the space-time where I can live.

Yes, I was in the fifth grade. Though I had entered elementary school one year late, the studies were hard for me and I always fell behind. But my classmates were supportive and friendly. The girls would call out, "Tommy, Tommy," and treat me like a doll to be played with. Though it's not something you should say about yourself, I was pretty cute then, and even today I think I am what you call handsome.

One day I was hanging around with a few girls in a corner of the schoolyard. I was caressing the hair of the girl next to me, when suddenly I got a surging sensation from the core of my body, and my underwear got wet. I was alarmed to discover that there is more than one way to wet your pants. After that it would happen to me once in a while even when I was alone. I would throw away the soiled briefs in the trash basket in my room, and eventually Mom found a pair. Oh, what a look on her face the moment she knew. Half crying, she pumped up her fortitude to declare, "You must absolutely never do this anywhere but in your own room. Otherwise I'll have to take you somewhere."

Mom repeated the same thing about three times, and then tears really started streaming from her eyes. I liked her face so much at that moment that, while I don't obey all of her orders, I have obeyed that one.

Anyway, my life in those days was just the best. My senses flourished. My class teacher, Tachikawa-sensei, was a young man whose countenance was crisp and firm, but yet somehow shadowed.

Mom and the other mothers, all in their thirties, suddenly exploded into PTA activity, and thought up all sorts of projects that would allow them to frequent the school. And on a parents' day, the place was packed.

Tachikawa-sensei bathed the whole class in his youthful enthusiasm. Everyone, from the star pupils at one end to me at the other, fell into his snare. Especially when he looked on an outsider like me, his eyes glowed brighter and their luminescence grew deeper. Though no one knew who first said it, he came to be called the Little Prince, and was the idol of the school.

All the classes were going to participate in the school recital with chorus, drama, or musical performances. My class decided to put on a play with a sci-fi flavor, *Somewhere on the Planet*. An unfailing egalitarian advocating class-wide participation in everything, the Little Prince created the role of the sun especially for me. Carrying a large sun I was to enter at stage right and walk across to stage left to a tune called *The Sun Rises, The Sun Sets*. Thinking that it was unnatural for the sun to move so fast, and that daytime needed the sun for a longer time, I would linger at the middle of the stage, which was apparently not right, so I had to do it over and over.

At the time, rumors spread that the Little Prince was having "an affair" with one of the mothers. It was said to be the mother of our leading lady, Izumi-san.

To tell the truth, I had a crush on Izumi herself. I loved her black hair that reached her shoulders—how often did I want to touch it? When I say I wanted to touch it, it was not with my hands but with my lips. I wanted to bundle up that smooth-flowing, seemingly alive and breathing hair, and press it down with my lips. I had long entertained that wish, but whenever I approached her she would turn around quickly with a wink or a smile that meant no.

It was her mother that was said to be having an affair with Tachikawa-sensei. I once heard Mom talking about it with other mothers.

"It's a one-way come-on from Izumi-san."

"That's terrible. People in the water trade move fast."

"Yes, I hear she works in a bar."

"They say her husband has heart trouble and has been in bed for quite a while."

"Ah, no wonder. . . ."

Their criticism was exclusively against Izumi's mother. When Mom talked about it, her voice overflowed with envy.

Performance day drew near and rehearsals entered the home-stretch, so the leading actress, Izumi, two other classmates, and I had to stay late after school. Our mothers were more than happy to come to school as self-appointed assistants. Of course Mom was milling around the gym, more jazzed up than usual.

I had to rehearse many times my walk across the stage, carrying the sun.

The Little Prince was coaching Izumi, his pale forehead glistening with perspiration. She had a long soliloquy to remember. Each time she moved her head her hair swayed. How many times did I feel the impulse to touch it with my lips?

The sun was supposed to appear after her monologue, so I was waiting in the wings in my coal-black costume, holding the big sun. From where I was standing I could see the graceful figure of the Little Prince, standing before the front-row seats, watching Izumi perform.

I was shifting my eyes back and forth between Izumi on the stage and the Prince on the floor, when I became aware of another powerful gaze pouring down on the Prince from a different direction.

Across the stage from me, in the opposite wing, stood a woman with her eyes fixed on the Prince. Though it was dark and we had the whole length of the stage between us, I could see beautiful beams of light emanating from her eyes.

Just as I was wishing I could touch Izumi's hair, the woman was longing to touch the Little Prince. It was Izumi's mother. Light from her body poured down on him, as if he were standing in a shower of gems. The moment I felt that, my head became numb.

On our way home, while Mom was gossiping with two other mothers about the affair, I suddenly blurted out,

"Today the year before last was Thursday. I wonder what day to-day last year was."

The two other mothers looked at me in surprise, then turned compassionate eyes toward Mom. She frowned slightly, but could afford to allow a little smile to play about her lips.

In the spring of the year when I became a sixth grader, Izumi's mother strangled her bed-ridden husband and then threw herself to her death from the fifth floor of the condo where they lived. Soon after that the Little Prince was transferred somewhere. The daughter also disappeared at about the same time.

Still today, when I see a longhaired woman I feel like drawing close to her. Mom strictly admonishes me against this, because if I do such a thing she will have to take me somewhere.

The poster drew in Seo-san, a company employee, Tatsumi-san, from a women's college, and Tomita-san, a middle school student, to make a total of sixteen of us in Blacaman. Our first production was *Count Dracula the Handsome*, to be directed by Tōta. I worried that if I had to carry the sun back and forth across the stage as many times as I did in the school play I would be worn out. But since Dracula belongs to the night, Tōta said, "Well, the moon might appear," which made me a bit nervous.

It would take almost two hours to perform *Count Dracula the Handsome*. Takeshi's mother made photocopies of the script for all the members. But for the four of us, thinking to save on copying cost, she made only one copy per family, and these she handed to the mothers. Her thinking was simple enough, but Mio objected.

"That's not right. Everyone is paying the same flat rate membership, so Tommy-san and the others should get their own copies."

This began a discussion that lasted all day. I thought it was okay either way, but all the students supported Mio. Seo, the company employee, was the only one to ask, "What's wrong with it? Mother and child can share one copy, can't they?" with a face that said this was only natural.

In situations like this, Mom has the bad habit of getting oddly feisty. To Takeshi's mother she said,

"Of course, Tommy and the others must get copies. We parents mustn't be so timid!"

In the end it was decided by majority vote that each member should get a copy of the script.

Casting was completed at the next meeting. Tōta, while maintaining a modest manner, made the decisions. Fat Takeshi would play the giant. Yōko, Yōji, and I would play phantoms, foreboding eeriness in the show. The role of the Count went to Seo. Saburo would play the salesman who got entangled in the nether world. Everyone was given a job on- or off-stage.

And Mom? She was the Witch! That decision energized her like nothing else.

Before that she had seemed displeased because Takeshi, as the giant, had a speaking role while I, as a ghost, would only walk. But when she got the role of witch, she looked satisfied. She quickly chose a jet-black dress and a golden lace shawl for her costume and, forgetful of me, began researching witches.

She began by buying a large picture book titled *The Witch's Handbook* written by one Malcolm Bird. It contained eleven lessons on how to become a witch, with everything from how to dress to how to make flying broomsticks. With its wonderful illustrations, it was an exhaustive guide rich in the know-how of day-to-day witchcraft. I was surprised to find myself opening this book on Mom's desk—I who had never read a book in my life.

Mom later learned that the entire troupe was adamant that only she and no one else had to play the witch. She told me this with a complex yet delighted expression.

Takeshi had got the role of giant because he was so fat, but was having a hard time memorizing his lines. Among the four of us he could read the fastest and the most accurately, but he was not good at learning things by heart, and his delivery was in a monotone. Tōta didn't know what to do.

Takeshi's mother would always take a seat in the corner of the room, and anxiously shift her gaze back and forth between the faces of the other troupe members and her son, as he recited his lines in the same monotone.

While that was going on I could understand what a fine person was Tōta, as he struggled so hard trying somehow to work it out. But the giant had so many appearances and so many lines that Mom and the other mothers put their heads together and concluded that it would be better if someone else took over the role. Mom broached the subject to Takeshi's mother.

"Yes, I've also been thinking that it's too much. It's a burden on Takeshi. Thank you for bringing it up. Ahhhhh—finally from tonight I can get some sleep."

And her voice really did sound as though a burden had been lifted from her shoulders. Tōta and Mom tried to console her, or rather to make excuses, saying it might have been all right if there had been more time, or if his lines had been slightly fewer. Still, Takeshi and his mother looked a little lonely and dejected.

So that's how it came about that the four of us all played ghosts together with Yōji's mother. Our costumes were black as coal from top to bottom. We danced to eerie music under ashen light.

"Tommy, all of you, one more try."

Mom, now a witch clad in black and gold, stood at Tōta's side noisily giving stage directions in his place.

The scene was only about three minutes long, but as we danced to the music over and over again my body became light and floated up into the air. It was as though my spirit too had flown out into a space somewhere and was wafting about. It was a delicious feeling.

Most likely I was dead.

"When do you die?"

I always used to ask that question to Mom.

"That 'you' should be 'I,' right? Why is it that you can't separate yourself from others? Why can't you understand such a simple word as that?"

I see. Mom takes it as a problem of language. She thinks that's all there is to it.

In the very depths of the depths of pitch-black space, Mom's gold lame flickers.

"Tommy, Tommy! OK, nothing to be done about it. You must be terribly tired, to go to sleep in a place like this."

Hearing Mom's voice off in the distance, I was drifting off into a dream.

4

THE SUMMER
NOBODY KNEW

I met Suma for the first time on the night of the Bon Festival.
There are two parks in the Larkhill district where I live. South
Park is near my home, and East Park is farther away. The annual Bon
Dance Festival alternates between these parks. It was the East's turn
this year.

On that day I left home nonchalantly around four o'clock in the
afternoon, when the district was just beginning to rustle and bus-
tle. As a Bon Dance–lover I wanted to check out the place in advance before Mom would say what she always said: "Don't go
early just to dally around. Seven o'clock at the earliest. After dinner."

But when I imagine the Bon Dance drumbeat, my body just naturally starts to move.

"Your Bon Dance—you have your own special style. It's like you're
rowing a boat. You just wave your body back and forth to the
rhythm."

Apparently Mom had come just once to see me dance, and that's
how she described my style.

"And you a thirty-year-old grownup—it's so embarrassing. Once
you get started, there's no stopping you. You even went into the middle of the circle. No, that kind of thing is not for me. The melodies
all sound the same—*don-doko, don-doko*. And the dances also all look

about the same. How people can get so devoted to such a thing is beyond me."

But I can understand those people.

Mom hadn't noticed that between the melodies that seemed the same, and between the motions of the arms and legs that seemed the same, there were delicate variations, so her opinion meant nothing.

"But this is the only festival of the year that you go to happy and uncomplaining, so I close my eyes to it."

That's why only at the Bon Festival I want to brush Mom off and get out as soon as I can. Not that I can dance nicely like other people. She's right about that. I swing to and fro and that's about it. But in fact my motions are subtly different with different songs.

Especially the sound of the drums has the power to lift my body from below the belly button. My body feels light, and I get an unbearably blissful feeling, as if I were being sucked away into an unknown universe.

That day Suma was sitting on a bench in the shade of a tree by the open space of the park where the dancing was to take place. She seemed to be idly gazing at the person working on the audio cables at the foot of the scaffolding, the children running around, and the early comers rehearsing the dances in their matching yukatas.

I love this scene, before the dancing starts. On this day the cherry trees, the stone steps and the sandboxes, which usually take command in the park, are relegated to the corners by the hanging lanterns and the loudspeakers bundled onto utility poles. It's as though they are waiting for a cue, while the women's excited voices fly about. I guess I come early against Mom's advice so I can dip myself into this atmosphere.

Apart from that, though, I had the feeling that the air around Suma's bench was entirely different.

I stood by the scaffold tower for a while, looking in her direction. Then suddenly she raised a white hand and beckoned to me.

It's my problem that I'm not good at communicating my ideas or thoughts, or talking about the real situation in real time. So if someone calls to me like that, I won't get the message. I tend to shift my eyes to a different direction or think of something totally irrelevant.

But not that day.

Suma smoothed her gray hair slightly upward and waved her hand toward me again. My legs began to move, and before I knew it I found myself standing in front of her.

Under the hot afternoon sun, people were drenched with sweat, but even between the deep lines on Suma's forehead not a drop could be seen. I sat next to her and watched the people going this way and that.

"Did you know? My father bought this lace dress for me. It was made in Paris," Suma said, holding up a sleeve of her dress. Loose threads were dangling from the frayed cuffs and hem. It was so abrupt that I reflexively turned toward her.

"I wonder where Paris is. I wonder if the bullet train stops there."

I knew there was a place called Paris from television.

"I don't think it does. Oh, yes, you must have come from far away too. Father used to come home from far-away places by boat. He always brought me *konpeitoh* sugar candies, and said, 'Here's something for you.' They came in glass bottles, and looked very pretty."

"*Konpei-toh, Eiffel-toh, kot-toh, sa-toh, kakkon-toh.*" I played with the words.

"Pfff . . ."

I felt she smiled faintly.

"You're Tommy, aren't you? I know that because people call you so. But your real name is Tomio, isn't it? I know everything about you."

The light from the setting sun fell on her gray hair and tinged it to a color like strawberry blond. It was so beautiful.

The lanterns were lit and more people came. Yet the air around Suma and me was colored differently.

"Suma. I'm Suma. Father liked her—the actress Sumako Matsui. I was told that was why."

There was no need to ask. Somehow I felt that I already knew her name, and knew her, from long before.

"What a big sun," she said.

Suma and I were looking beyond the uproar rising before us at the sun going down behind the roof of a house.

"Ladies and gentlemen, let's dance and have a good time. Larkhill's annual Bon Festival is . . ."

After women and men took turns speaking into the microphone, the drum on the stage began to boom and the yukatas, with their patterns of waves in light blue against a white background, began to move in a circle.

"Haaaaaah . . ."

A square-faced man with bushy eyebrows put his hands under his sash and pumped up his chest. As his high-pitched, feminine voice echoed, his face got redder and redder from the neck up. As I watched this my body, still seated on the bench, began to sway.

I noticed that words were spilling from the mouth of Suma sitting by me.

"Haaahh-aaah-iih, across the mountains, are birds migrating? Clouds are aaaahh-iih, clouds are gathering. Come, Oku-Chichibu, yo-ii-yo-ii-yoo-iiya-sah. Flowery Nagatoro, those tables of rock. Who will you meet under the pale foggy moon?"

This was definitely not the song being sung on the stage. In fact she sang almost without melody but just occasionally hit high notes, then would take a breath so that the lyric broke off.

With wrinkles converging around her mouth as she opened it wide to sing, Suma looked like a little girl. I too felt like a five-year-old again. My heart skipped.

"Come summer, the rose and azalea bloom. Weavers of Chichibu Meisen silk finish stowing their autumn worms and sowing their wheat, and wait for the Chichibu Night Fest . . ."

She sang for a while, and then staggered to her feet. I was raptly swaying when she squeezed my hand. The bones nearly collapsed in my palm. I stopped mechanically.

She limped toward the ring of dancers, leaning to one side, probably because her white slippers had been unevenly worn out. This time I was the one who took her hand and led the way.

Some women who were dancing flashed censorious eyes at us, but we did not care at all, and cut through to the center, right by the scaffold.

Then Suma became another person. Her slouchy back straightened up smoothly, her feet got neatly aligned, and her right foot gave a tap to the ground. With that the fingers of her left hand arranged themselves gracefully and rose to point to the sky. Then her right hand. She danced like nobody else around us, but it looked beautiful to me.

Generally I'm not good at imitating people, but swept away by Suma's dance I found myself waving my arms, moving my legs, and rocking my body.

Yes, that reminds me. I was five years old. I was expelled by a nursery near our home just when I ended my first semester there, because, they said, they could no longer take care of me. Mom then sought advice from the doctor who knew me well. He introduced us to a kindergarten far away.

Mom and I commuted there every day. It took an hour and a half, and we had to change trains twice.

"It's natural that there are many kinds of children. Just relax and come to us. It will work out."

The big director of the kindergarten accepted us as though he was holding us tightly in his arms.

Thinking nothing of the rush-hour crush, I would be on the same train every morning, standing at the very front of the lead car and staring straight ahead. I would not do my usual soliloquy, but my eager eyes would be riveted on the never-ending tracks, I in a state of solitary ecstasy.

Mom would be looking out the windows, knowing I would stay calm while we were on the train.

"Are you taking him to an elite school at this early age? So much trouble, and every day! And you have to accompany him there and back."

I heard this female voice, plainly irritated and sarcastic, implying that it was unwarranted to bring me on such a jam-packed train. The woman probably took the same train every day. Mom whipped around, but could find no words and was silent, with an ambiguous smile.

"Aaaahh, she doesn't understand anything. She knows nothing about other people's troubles. But then, that's all right too. Tommy taken for an elite boy?—not bad. You do look handsome dressed up in that uniform. Uh-huh . . ." Mom mused aloud after we got off.

A miracle happened at that kindergarten, or so Mom said. In less than ten days after we started going there, I took to joining the morning fitness exercises in the playground. Believe it or not I started moving my limbs just like the other children.

After that I clicked castanets at recitals and copied pictures that Mayumi-chan, the girl next to me, drew of her mother's face. Mom was ecstatic because, though I had drawn pictures before, I had never done a portrait.

However, I am not made to pile up efforts to become better at things. A thing is just a thing for me: an ephemeral snippet of experience. And that's the problem. Even though I may learn things one by one, they don't get integrated inside me.

Mom knew that, so while she was chokingly thanking the Director, surely somewhere deep in her heart there remained a dark shadow.

My past experiences are cut up like photo slides, each detailing a separate scene. I soothe myself by extracting one of them that will somehow fit the situation that I am up against.

So now I was back in kindergarten. Suma was my teacher. I was at her heels, flapping my arms and twisting my body. Someone on the stage stared at us with an accusatory look for a while. Past experience had made me sensitive to that sort of thing, so I could detect it right away. But luckily neither one of us felt like responding.

Suma and I kept on dancing.

Then suddenly her shoulders rolled to one side, her body folded down, and she collapsed to the ground. Alarmed, I looked at her, tried to help her to her feet, but she only shook her head faintly. A couple of ladies came running.

"What happened?"

"Are you all right?"

"Yes, yes, I'm all right. Could you please help me home?"

Suma's voice was unexpectedly firm. Two men came over and, supporting her by the arms, helped her out of the circle. I followed them. The drumbeat, after waning a moment, resumed even louder, and surrounded by that sound, the three of them exited the park into the dark streets. Now and then the men's voices encouraging Suma reached my ears through the terribly hot air.

They entered a bungalow at the edge of the residential area. I stood by the hedge for a while, and then, because I felt Suma's pale hand had beckoned me, entered.

"I'm all right, I'm all right. Thank you. Oh, Tommy's here."

Suma had slumped down on the elevated threshold of the entrance hall and spoke in a musical voice when she recognized me. The two men looked from one to the other of us, and then left.

"Come in, come in. I'm glad you came. I'm all right now."

She got to her feet leaning against the shoe-cupboard and walked inside. While taking off my shoes, I felt I heard Mom's voice: "It's this late, and you're still hanging around. It's about time you came home."

Paying no attention to that, I followed Suma. She turned on the light. The room was full of things: a bed, a bookshelf, a sofa, a desk, and three chairs. A lot of French dolls in antiquated dresses were placed side by side in a glass cabinet in a corner of the room.

"Sit down there, in that chair. I've turned on the air conditioner. It'll be cool soon."

Perhaps feeling a little better, she laid herself down on the bed.

"Where is this? I wonder if the bullet train stops at Paris."

"Oh, yes, it was Paris. *Un appartement en Paris.*"

Taken with a slight fit of coughs, she pressed her right hand against her throat. Under the chair I was sitting on, I saw something strange—a dead cockroach.

"When you clean a room, you clean its corners. Look at these balls of dust."

I imagined Mom holding a vacuum.

"If I don't say anything, you do abominably sloppy work. The basics of cleaning are tight, trim, and tidy. Remember the triple T."

Mom had started to lecture me like that after I entered middle school as though she wanted to make a janitor of me. More than twenty years later I am no better with the triple T, or the double or the single T for that matter. I guessed that Suma also might not be so good at cleaning, with something like a dried cockroach lying in her room.

The drumbeat and the merrymaking reached us like breaking waves.

"Haaah-aaah-ii, when the moon stands high above the stage, the dancers surround it with ten rings, twenty rings . . ."

Mumbly words were spilling out of Suma's mouth.

"Father, don't walk so fast!"

Suddenly she bolted upright on the bed and cried out. It was a shrill, childish voice.

"When we would go to our house in the mountains of Chichibu, Father was not himself. Why? When we went to that big house with the thatched roof deep in the mountains, I would ask him, 'What souvenir can we bring Mother this time?' I tried hard to talk about Mother, who had either been in the hospital or lying in the back room of our home ever since I was born. And yet, and yet, in that house in the mountains, Father . . ."

Her voice trembled in agitation.

"When Father came back from a far away country, he would spend half the month by Mother's side and the other half up there in Chichibu. He always took me with him. Look, we can already see it . . . that woman quietly standing by the big zelkova tree. She's Aunt Ito. Father pounds the earth as he climbs the hill. He pulls my hand so hard I'm afraid he might rip it off . . . it was all I could do to keep up with him, my legs tangling. But I did try to lean backward intentionally, pulling against his hand. And yet it seemed some power was welling up inside him."

"Does the bullet train stop in Chichibu or not?"

I demanded this because Suma's face had begun to contort as though she were desperately bearing something.

"I hate you, Father!"

She screamed shrilly.

"Does it or doesn't it!?"

I yelled back because now I really was burning to know whether the bullet train stopped at Chichibu.

Then I felt a ferocious glance from Suma. Somehow I began to feel sad. I tried to pick up the roach at my feet and put it on the table, but it broke into pieces on the way and fell like a bunch of dust to the floor. All I had left in my hand was one of its legs, so I just put that on the table.

"Come summer, roses and azaleas bloom. Weavers of the Chichibu Meisen silk . . ."

She started to sing again.

"Does the bullet train stop in Chichibu or not!?"

I was startled by the loudness of my voice.

She stared at me for the first time.

"Smoke is rising. Trains that put out smoke stop there. The bullet train doesn't. Don't worry, Tommy."

That was a peaceable voice.

She got out of the bed and stood up. Then she stretched the fingers of both hands, raised them over her head, and set them to dancing.

"Haaaahh-aaah-ii, weavers of the Chichibu Meisen silk, stow the autumn worms and finish sowing wheat . . ."

In the thin space by the bed, Suma sang, taking a step forward and then a half-step back. Every move she made was perfect. Because her hands waved as if beckoning to me, I stood up without thinking and faced her.

Suma raised her chin, squared her chest and shoulders, and sang with all her might.

" . . . Clouds are . . . aaahh-ii . . . clouds are gathering. Come, Oku Chichibu, yo-ii-yo-ii-yo-iiya-sah . . ."

Overpowered, I fell backward and sat down on the bed. She took my hand and lifted me back to my feet. I started moving again, but then she sank down to the bed with a gasp.

"Aaah-ah. Tommy, sorry, but could you bring me some tea? It's in the refrigerator. There's a glass too."

I was dancing as if nothing had happened, but because she kept drooping I started to worry, and went to fetch the tea. Weaving my way around the bookshelf and newspapers and clothes scattered around the chairs, I brought her a glass of barley tea. She took three sips of tea, returned the glass to me, and then lay back on the bed. "Let me have a rest."

Suddenly the drumbeat roared loud in my ears. I held up my wristwatch to the desk lamp. It was sixteen minutes past eight. By now Mom must be engrossed in a movie on television. I've made it a rule on Bon Dance night to come home every year at ten sharp, so I was still in a safe range of time.

I could tell from her breathing that Suma had dozed off, which enticed me to curl up as well. Though the bed was spacious, her pint-sized body slid right into the dent created by my weight.

"Oh, you're tired too."

She wasn't quite asleep, for she opened her eyes slightly and jerked herself closer to the headboard.

"Sleep well. Sweet dreams."

She stroked my hair with her tiny hand.

"In the house in the Chichibu mountains, Ito hugged me like this and stroked my bobbed hair like this. She had a nice scent, it was cozy in her bosom, but I was feeling fiercely rebellious. I wanted to run away and go back to Mother. I pushed desperately at Ito's chest to get free, but she wouldn't let me go. After a while I would surrender to the comfort of her embrace and fall asleep."

Suma's hand stopped rubbing my head.

"Because, because . . ."

She broke into a sob.

"Because Mother's illness was contagious, so I had no memory of her treating me like that."

Suddenly her trembling voice was muffled, tightly pressed against my head.

"I hate Father."

I kept still for some time, but was unable to suppress my pain and anxiety. I blurted out, "When do you die?"

"Look, there you go again, calling yourself 'you.' You really wanted to say, 'When do I die?' didn't you? If you were talking about something else it wouldn't matter, but when you're talking about death, you can really shock the other person. The word 'you' means the person near you, the person that you are looking at at the time. You're over thirty now—it's puzzling. You are pretty capable at other things, but you still don't get a thing as simple as that."

Mom's nagging became nearly audible.

"Oh, yes. I'm always thinking about that. Tommy, you are so kind to care about me."

Suma was back to her regular voice.

"Yes, it's about time I decide when to die. Look, my heart is wondering whether it should stop or not."

She abruptly pushed me away, sat up on the bed, and began to unbutton her dress. The six buttons seemed too tight, so I lent a hand.

The desk lamp cast a shadow on her thin and pallid bosom. A withered pair of breasts spilled out with the nipples pointing downward.

Face to face with me, she took my hand and placed it under her left breast.

"See? It's about ready to take a rest—my heart."

Buried in her slack skin, her eyes flashed momentarily.

This was the first time I had ever seen a naked woman so close. The breasts felt flaccid and forlorn, but their nipples tickled the balls of my fingers when she spoke.

"Father, please don't go away again."

Suma shrank down and hurled herself against my chest. Her force knocked me down on the bed, with her on top.

I threw my arms about her, and rolled over sideways. Her convulsive sobs and the touch of her hair on my jaw felt so pleasant that I wanted to shout.

"Father, Father."

Murmuring, she buried her nails into my chest.

At which moment my whole body became a pillar of fire, and something hot spurted out from my underbelly. Then all the strength went out of me. I tossed Suma to one side, and stretched out on my back.

After a while she noticed the state I was in.

Saying only, "Oh, my," she crouched over the edge of the bed, took out tissue paper from below, and wiped the stuff away.

It was a casual "Oh, my," as though she had been taking a walk and met someone she hadn't seen for a while.

That thing first occurred when I was a fifth-grader. When Mom came to know it she said, "This is allowed only in your room and nowhere else, absolutely."

She said this in an unusually awkward way. Tears rolled from her eyes, and I was more surprised by her intensity than I was about the thing itself.

Compared to that, Suma's nonchalance was amazing.

Suddenly the skin on my stomach became twitchy. For some reason it all seemed funny, and I began to laugh.

Suma, by my side, began to breathe evenly in sleep.

Maybe the drummer was getting tired, for the drumbeat was slowing down.

I was drifting off into a comfortable drowsiness while recalling things from the past.

The bed was, no, it wasn't soft like this. It was a hard spring bed. When I entered elementary school, I never wanted to enter my classroom, and would hang out in the nurse's office.

The first thing I would do in the morning at school was to play on the swing and the slide for a while. When the bell chimed, all the pupils would go to their classrooms, and I would go to the nurse's office.

My teacher, Umino-sensei, was a woman of steady character, and Mom had primed her about me before my admission, so she always saw to it that I would do the things that the other children did insofar as possible. So she was worried when I didn't enter the classroom. She would come with my classmates to get me, but I stubbornly refused to go. In the nurse's room I would keep on jumping up and down on the bed, just like on a trampoline. The hopping and bouncing gave me a physical sensation that was irresistibly refreshing.

One day Umino-sensei said, "If you like it so much, so be it. Let's bring the bed into the classroom. Kashiwagi-kun, you will work on the bed instead of in a chair. All right?" She talked to me holding my shoulders and looking straight into my eyes.

I suddenly felt something between ticklish and itchy around my belly button. After Umino-sensei told her about the plan, Mom was uncharacteristically timid. "Well, I'm afraid to go to school. What will the other mothers think? . . . Though I'm so grateful to her for her thoughts."

"In return, Kashiwagi-kun, I want you to promise me. From the second semester, from September, the bed will be returned to the nurse's room, and you will sit in a chair. Do you understand me?"

Umino-sensei said that over and over again, looking me in the face.

When I went to school the next day, five or six girls from my class were waiting for me, and dragged me into the classroom. The big bed stood imposingly in the very back.

I flinched for a moment, but, thinking that Umino-sensei had been so kind as to have it brought in, I stayed on it the whole day.

Stretched out on the bed and watching sideways, I came to know that a classroom was a place where teachers wrote letters on the blackboard, pupils raised their hands, and various other things went on.

From time to time Umino-sensei would look toward me and call my name: "Kashiwagi-kun."

Parents' visitation day was always hard on Mom. Joined by rows of Education Moms in the rear of the classroom, she still looked ahead undaunted. Only I was aware of her bottomless solitude and loneliness. To root for her I kept jumping up and down on the bed.

In September the bed was returned to the nurse's room as promised and I began to sit in a chair. It seemed strange even to me.

I still remember the names of all my classmates, the smell of the classroom, and Umino-sensei's face with its dimpled smile. I can quickly pick these out of my precious memory cabinet and spread them out before me.

Immersed in memories so far back in time, it seems I slept for a while. I woke up to find Suma seated in a chair, putting up her hair.

I have long held an obsession about women's hair. It's not about pretty or becoming hairdos. My body is somehow attracted by hair itself. That's why I abruptly kiss it instead of just touching it or looking at it. The very feel of hair on my lips stimulates my five senses and spreads a delicate pleasure through my whole body.

When I was in middle school, I used to approach the girls, and sometimes they would turn around and say, "No! Your eyes are after my hair," or they might tilt their heads and say, "OK, but just a little."

"Remember that you are grown up. You must never do that. No matter how much I'm your mother, I couldn't take responsibility for you. I'd have to send you away to some distant place."

Against Mom threatening me with tear-filled eyes, I had no chance of winning. And yet for the past thirty years this had been to me a kind of frustration and discontent, like looking for a toilet forever in a dream. So when Suma frankly and forcibly pressed her hair on to me, I could only surrender to her. Also to her immensely natural kindness.

Suma smoothed her hair, buttoned up her lace dress, and was silent for a while. She seemed to be letting her thoughts drift in the distance.

Yes, she must be thinking about the old days. I could relate to that. She's like me. She brings memories of things past up into her mind, and uses them as a means of living in the present.

I am not able to forecast the future or make sense of present reality as well as others do, but on the other hand, I remember the past very well, especially the things from my childhood. I bring up the memories of past experiences and lay them over the present reality, as my way of understanding and accepting it.

Suma had a way of talking softly for a while, then suddenly changing to a childish voice, or shifting to a completely different subject. My bet was that Mom would snap at her just like she does at me: "Don't say irrelevant things."

"When the moon stands high over the tower . . . Aunt Ito taught me how to dance. On Bon Festival nights Father used to come with us to the village square. When the three of us were together, I would feel terribly lonely and somehow upset, and would intentionally go astray or hide in the shadow of a tree. Each time I did that they would both look all over for me, but as I watched them it seemed as though they were enjoying it like a game, which made my heart still more stubborn. There were times when he would leave me with Aunt Ito and go away for three days or so. I hated having to stay with her and her parents. Except for Aunt Ito, everybody there kept a distance from me as if I were an abscess not to be touched. They paid no attention to me no matter what I did. Maybe Father had asked her—if I didn't wash my hands and face or if I slept late, she would get upset and tag behind me all day long. When that happened I would think, shall I do something really mean to her, or should I go all out and fawn on her?"

Suma went on and on in a monotone, as if she were reading aloud. Only when she said Ito, would her voice flinch slightly.

I was listening lying on the bed, halfway giving in to drowsiness, so I was calm enough to understand well what she was saying.

"When Father was away I had a good appetite. But I didn't like to eat much when he was around. I ate everything Ito cooked for me when he was away. But when he was around, I didn't eat at all. That seemed to weigh heavily on her mind as she sat next to Father with his troubled face. He never brought any presents from overseas for her. Though he did buy lots of presents, like embroidered nightgowns and pillow cases for Mother and dresses and sweets for me."

I noticed that Suma had been plucking at threads from the edge of the bed sheet and shredding them. It seems she was pretty strong. The shreds were dropping to the floor, making it whitish.

"I wonder what month and what day next year's Bon Festival will be."

Maybe under Mom's influence, I liked cleanliness. I asked about the date because I was annoyed by the shreds amassing on the floor.

And this time my words were on target.

"Yes, the Bon Dance was on August 3. Aunt Ito danced beautifully. She was the best in the village."

She stopped pulling at the linen and looked as though she were gazing far away.

Great! I was great! I did communicate my thought to her, that she should stop pulling the sheet. How I wished Mom were there to see this. But maybe not. She wouldn't be impressed at all. She would dismiss it, saying, "There you go again, saying something irrelevant. You just cannot have a conversation. Pitiful!"

No, Mom, you're not getting it. Even though I can't have a conversation, I still want to communicate the true feelings at the bottom of my heart to other people.

Suma stood up and started dancing again. She moved her thin body forward, then backward, held out her hands, then pulled them back. Her style was so neat that it seemed she was about to stop the flow of air around her. After a little while she sat down and resumed talking.

"Ito took my hand and brought me to the festival. She was so pretty she was glowing that evening. I knew that her entire body was conscious of Father, who was slowly walking behind us. Dressed in my yukata with red goldfish printed on it, I resisted Ito and pulled against her hand. 'No, no, I don't want to go,' I protested. But actually, actually, I was delighted and wanted to rush to the square as quickly as possible and have Father see me dance. Actually I wanted to run ahead, leading her by the hand. Actually, actually . . ."

She was in tears. "Actually, actually . . ." It felt like her trembling voice was beating me all over my body. Actually, actually, she loved Aunt Ito. Yes, maybe Suma's "actually . . ." should be followed by, "I loved her."

"The Bon Festival is what day, what month, what year?"

Typically, I blurted a question about a date.

"In the middle of the Taisho Era, August 3, the festival took place on August 3, every year. Seventy years, or more, have passed. Oh, no, that was the year before last."

I perfectly understood her. Suma lived by drawing out the threads of her memory and chewing them over and over. She was just like me. When I thought this, a feeling of closeness and nostalgia for her welled up from the bottom of my heart.

I could hear the drumbeat from afar.

Gently I went around to touch her hair with my lips from behind. This is my most affectionate form of expression toward a person.

Her gray hair smelled of soy sauce. She was seated as if buried in the chair, muttering and sniffling.

"After Mother passed away, Father begged me to let Aunt Ito come and live with us, but I refused. I rebelled against her through and through. Because I felt sorry for Mother, bedridden ever since I was old enough to know. . . . No, that wasn't it. I was afraid of loving Ito even more. If that happened, Father would then feel free to become more intimate with her—that's what I couldn't bear. I wanted to attract his attention to me. I was jealous of her."

When I do my monologue, Mom always scolds me, but Suma's monologue-like words opened up a little gateway into my narrow heart, and reverberated through it. That's probably because she was speaking out her true feelings that had been tucked away deep inside her.

Yes, that's the point, Mom. When you express your true feelings, it becomes a monologue. It's just that in my case this happens more frequently and more unexpectedly than with others. Now I understand: soliloquy is the way you talk when you speak the truth. But I still don't have the words to let Mom know of this discovery. That's the big problem for me.

"Aaaa, life is no fun. It's full of loneliness, isn't it?"

Suma's tone suddenly shifted.

"Aaaa, it's as if I was born to be lonely."

She tottered to her feet, turned off the air conditioner and opened a window.

"Tommy, come over here. The new moon is out."

Standing beside her, I looked at the crescent moon.

Without our noticing it, the drumbeat had ceased. The sky was quiet and dark.

"I have a good idea, Tommy. On the next full moon evening, we'll go to the river. I will make a hundred dumplings with a name on each of them. Ito taught me this. You can get your wish, whatever it is. I'll make them for you, dumplings with your name on them."

Suma went into the kitchen and came back with a pretty basket full of candies. She appeared to be feeling better.

"Soon after Mother passed away, Father was killed in a shipwreck. I was ten years old. After that I went to live with Father's parents."

Seated in a chair, she began talking again.

Her storytelling manner was very changeable. She would suddenly shift to a childlike voice and manner, then go back to sounding like an ordinary old woman.

"I don't remember why, but after that I visited the house in the Chichibu mountains once. It was the day before the full moon. And four days later Ito was to marry into a family far away. She made a hundred cute little dumplings from rice flour. She wrote with sumi our names, Ito and Suma, on each one of them. The next day she and I walked to a nearby river. The full moon was beautifully reflected in the water. Nobody else was around. We sat down on the riverbank and floated the dumplings one by one. I was to wish a wish, one and only one wish, in my heart. Ito said it would surely be granted. I knew what her wish was. I'm sure she was longing to see Father once more. I thought so, and that's why I prayed hard to be able to see Mother once more. But actually, actually, I didn't care at all about Mother because her illness had kept me from getting close to her."

Suma's face, which had blushed for a moment, crumpled back into wrinkles.

"The next full moon will be September 9, the Harvest Moon. Because today is August 16. Let's meet at seven. I'll make the dumplings and wait for you, Tommy. Think about your wish, okay?"

Soon after, I walked home, down the deserted streets, accompanied by the moon.

Mom seemed to have fallen asleep watching television, and welcomed me with a big yawn.

I could hardly wait for the ninth of September. Every day I pored over the lunar phase chart in the weather report in the newspaper.

The moon grew bigger little by little. I watched the sky every night. It was fun, because I love things connected with the sun and the moon. There, nothing ever goes wrong and nothing ever changes. The one thing I could trust, and predict with certainty, was the waxing and waning of the moon.

"Why can't you engage with people with the same enthusiasm you have for the sun and the moon? For goodness' sake . . ."

Since I was spending many hours outside the house watching sunsets and night skies, Mom was amply sarcastic.

"People are bound to change their minds minute by minute. You fear that, and believe only in the laws of the universe. That might sound cool, but actually you're taking the easy way out. It's not fair. Can't you stand in my shoes once in a while?"

Just once I went and stood outside Suma's house during the day. In the deadly still air, I could feel her breathing.

September 9. I kept my promise and stood in front of her house at seven sharp.

But something was out of the ordinary.

People were coming and going. I took a step into the hall and heard the sound of hushed voices.

"It seems it was sudden. A housewife in the neighborhood found her. I'm told she had collapsed in the hall, already gone. It was early this morning."

"The poor thing. How sad to die alone."

Dead. Suma was dead. I stood paralyzed in the hall.

"Yes, it's about time I decide when to die. Look, my heart is wondering whether it should stop or not."

Suma's voice from the other day echoed.

Mom once said, when I repeated, "When do you die?" "There you go again. You said 'you' again. What you really want to know is when you yourself will die, don't you? But no one knows. Death comes from nowhere. When a person is dead, that means that wherever you go, and however much you search, you can't find that person again. Everyone is bound to disappear in the end."

Suma was dead. No matter where I looked for her, there was no Suma who had cried pressing her gray hair against my chest. No longer was there Suma who would raise her poised hands to dance.

Then I spotted a parcel wrapped in cloth on the shoe cabinet. I opened it right away. Yes, the dumplings were in it. I grabbed the bundle with both hands and dashed out.

Suma made these cakes, brought the bundle to the hall, then disappeared.

But tonight was the full moon, the night she was to go to the river with me.

I walked along in a trance. The moon followed me, looking as though it was about to fall to the earth.

"When is the next full moon?"

"What happened to Suma? She died. She died."

Words flew out of my mouth in quick succession: a flood of monologue.

From time to time I stopped to look up at the moon. Suddenly my heart brimmed over with the wish to see her again.

I broke into a run. I ran holding the pack tight so the dumplings wouldn't fall out.

The small river was waiting for me just outside the residential area, a shaky moon floating on its surface. I reached the waterside, sat on a stone, and unfolded the cloth. A hundred white dumplings were jostling in a bamboo colander. On each one the name "Tommy" was written in black.

One by one, one by one, I began dropping them into the stream. Splash, splat, the dumplings would bob back up, dance, and quickly go on their way. *"You can get your wish, whatever it is."*

I heard Suma's voice. Yes.

"I wish you would come back to me once more. Suma. I wish the bullet train would stop . . ."

Again and again I whispered toward the ribbon of white dumplings that was moving off into the distance.

Look, there's Suma!

On my way back I raised my eyes and saw her dancing in the round moon.

5

TUNNELS

A woman had been killed.

On a path leading to the woods right near the Larkhill district where I live, she laid face down, dead.

Unfortunately it happened on a Saturday, which is why she wasn't found sooner.

That path is a shortcut to the bus stop, so on a weekday she would have been found early in the morning by the people going to work, but as it was she wasn't found until close to noon by a passing housewife. The police investigation indicated that the woman was in the middle of the woods when she was stabbed in the back, and that she had crawled out to the path before she died—just like in a TV thriller.

She was stabbed at around six in the morning, so if she had been found sooner, she might have been saved.

We moved to Larkhill when I was five. In the twenty-five years since then there hasn't even been talk of a theft in this place, let alone a murder, so the whole community was in an uproar.

I don't exactly understand what "killing somebody" means. But it's probably something hard for anybody to explain.

Mom talked about the incident forever with the women in the neighborhood, but I guess it wasn't enough, because in the evening she even started badgering me about it while I was fixing dinner.

"A woman was killed. She was stabbed in the chest. Do you understand what I'm saying?"

Even though she knew it was me, who as usual was not going to give her an ordinary response, still today Mom's tension got higher and higher.

"What will happen to her two children? One is in high school and the other is in middle school. She was forty-three, she had everything ahead of her."

She pulled a chair out from under the table and sat down.

"They say the bleeding was terrible. The knife went in through her back and reached her heart."

"I wonder what day of the week Saturday this week is."

Suddenly, my top-special question sprang from my lips.

Mom glanced sidelong up to my face with her oh-not-again look, gave a big sigh, spread out her arms wide, and then stood up and shrugged her shoulders like an American.

"Saturday will definitely fall on Saturday."

She spat out the answer, probably the kindest she could muster after having been interrupted. I began chopping an onion, humming a tune.

For me, fixing my favorite fried rice was more important than talk about the slain woman.

I am thirty years old, but for me the hardest thing is to communicate what I am thinking in a way that it can be understood. The harder I try, the more my answers seem to go against the others' expectations, and they give me strange looks, or laugh, or are unable to conceal the pity that comes oozing out of them. "So you can immediately come up with the day of the week New Year fell on last year, or tell us the titles of the annual TV history dramas for the last twenty-five years—that doesn't get you anywhere. Can't you just carry on a normal conversation?" Mom always grumbles at me like this, but those are my special pleasures, whereas engaging with people, understanding them, for me that's very, very hard.

I guess I just haven't been able to find the right language to tell people what I really feel. So these questions and expressions, which Mom says are irrelevant and strange, keep bubbling out.

For all that I like to cook, and when I cook something in my repertoire like fried rice, fried noodles, meatballs or hamburgers, they taste pretty good. Mom takes advantage of that, and even though she will sometimes complain and say "This is pretty greasy" or something, still when it fits her schedule she will have me cook.

"She lived on the farthest corner of Larkhill, you know, way before you get to the bakery, Mrs. Tōno, she's the one who got killed."

Mom sat back down in the chair, folded her arms, and started at me again.

I turned my head to the ceiling to prevent the tears, brought on by the onion, from running down my cheeks, and moved only my hands.

"To kill somebody is, well, it's hard if you suddenly have to explain it."

Mom was also looking upward, thinking.

"To kill someone is . . . there's a person in front of you, different from yourself, and you suddenly cut off that person's life. Do you understand what I am saying?"

I didn't understand very well, but I wondered if it had something to do with dying.

"When do you die?"

I ventured the question while putting the onion, now all in tiny pieces, into a bowl. My face was blubbery with tears.

"There you go again. Your 'you' means yourself, right? Ah, it's so complicated. I mean, what you wanted to ask was, 'When will I die' wasn't it? To be thirty and not understand such a simple thing, it's pitiful, really."

Mom's sigh was more exaggerated than usual, but then suddenly her face became serious.

"But maybe this time your 'you' really meant me. Suddenly it came to me. It's because of that incident."

"Poor Mrs. Tōno. She's dead. She wasn't sick, somebody killed her."

To be killed. I don't understand that. But I think I have some idea of what it is to die. I don't tend to think much about the future, and I live by juxtaposing myself in the present with myself in the past.

Vaguely, I think that when I am no longer able to do that is when I will die.

But to be killed, that I don't understand. I don't understand the "to be."

I mumbled some words I'd heard on TV.

"To be loved, to be loved. To be killed, to be killed."

"Eh? What's that you said?"

Mom unfolded her arms and stood up. It seemed that she wanted to get a look at my face, but I had turned on the gas and was pouring oil into the frying pan.

For some reason Mom was silent for a moment with a complicated expression, and then she asked me again.

"You said, 'to be loved'? You said 'to be killed'?"

"To be loved" and "to be killed" had somehow seemed the same to me.

I put the chopped onion and minced pork into the frying pan. They made a lively sound, and flames shot up. At that moment Mom stretched out her hand and turned off the gas. Then with the same hand she grabbed my shoulder and turned me around to face her.

"To be loved, to be killed. Good words! For you, very good. That's the first time in your life you've used those words. Good, good, because to be loved, to be killed, you need another person. You need someone beside yourself. Hooray!"

Mom gave a big cheer, and then took hold of the sides of my mouth and pulled them apart hard. Then she turned on the gas again.

I shook the pan as it began sputtering again.

To heap steaming fried rice into a slightly convex, snow-white plate is pure delight. But today Mom had willfully turned off the gas and interrupted my cooking just when I was getting into it, destroying my mood and ruining my appetite.

When something like that happens, it triggers one of my bad habits. I can't stop myself. Unhappy memories from the past, times when I was harshly scolded rise up into my head and words start pouring out of my mouth.

Mom put her face flat on the table.

According to Mom, when I go into this state my vocabulary gets very rich, and I rattle on about one incident after another, no matter how long ago they happened. She says I imitate the voices and the manner of speaking of others so well that it gives you the strange feeling that it really is those others who are speaking.

"Really, Tommy, what is it like inside your head?"

As my monologue storm subsided, Mom raised her head.

"Tommy" is the nickname that Mom got from my name, Tomio.

As she picked up her spoon, sniffling, there were tears in her eyes. But my tears from the onion had dried up long before.

A week passed, but the killer had not been found.

Whenever and wherever Mom met any neighbor that's what they talked about.

"Don't you think one of those people did it?"

"Yes, yes, some of them have such strange looks in their eyes."

"I hear most of them are on medication. So when the effects wear off, a person can snap."

"I don't think so. Statistically the crime rate is lower for people with that kind of illness than for the general population."

Mom's defense of "those people" came in an, for her, unusually feeble voice.

Their workshop had been built in the middle of the rice paddies behind Larkhill.

People who simply cannot find work in ordinary companies. People who, even if they do find work, can't get along on the job. Here with the help of doctors and instructors, they were doing a variety of jobs. There were about ten of them commuting to work there.

Two years ago when the plan was being proposed, approval of the local residents was required, and so many meetings of the town association were held.

Seventy percent of the residents were against the project, with some ten percent spearheading the opposition.

This put Mom, with me as her misfit son, in a painful position. But maybe because pain itself can be a kind of strength, Mom rolled up her sleeves, sometimes encouraging herself by muttering, "This is just the kind of situation where I need to act."

My philosophy is "wrap yourself in something long," which means keep quiet and play it safe, so when Mom goes into her campaign mode, I can't stand getting hit by the spray.

"How many days does February have next year?"

What I meant to say by this question was "Cool down, cool down," but she ignored me.

The town association held many meetings.

"Of course it would be best if everybody could hold regular jobs at regular places, and we wouldn't need to build special facilities . . ." Mom would head off for meetings sometimes grumbling, sometimes arguing with herself.

Mrs. Kawabata who lives nearby is Mom's close friend, and she occasionally drops by for lunch.

"Well, I don't care what anybody says, it's just terrible. Saying, 'With those people here we can't let our daughters out of the house,' or 'We have to think of our children.' It's just too much."

"You're right. But still, that's the way most people think. Nobody knows what those people are really like. I might have some of the same feelings myself, deep down, some awful prejudice. But I don't announce it at public meetings. Am I being dishonest?"

Mrs. Kawabata stuck out the tip of her tongue and shrugged her shoulders.

"Oh, don't talk like that. But I also might have a thought somewhere in my mind like, 'My boy isn't like them.'"

"But wasn't that one just too awful? 'If we allow in something like that, the land prices will go down.' Who does he think he is? That's a violation of human rights."

The two ate and talked on and on before Mrs. Kawabata went home.

"Ladies and gentlemen. I have lived here in Larkhill for ten years now. Thanks to you my son, whom you all know about, has been able to live here freely and happily. People should be able to live and work where they like, no matter who, no matter where. These people who are coming, I think they would all rather find a regular job in a company somewhere. But they just can't. So they are trying to learn how to work, helping each other. The land has been purchased. I don't think anybody can say, *You can't build such and such. Do this! Do that!* Most of you may only be thinking of how, if these people come, it will damage the image of Larkhill, but please try to look at it from a different angle. Welfare is going to become an important issue. How would it be if we switched over to this positive image: Larkhill, a town compassionate to the elderly and the socially disadvantaged? Larkhill, a town warmhearted to all. I think that would be marvelous."

Mom had stood up out of her chair, and after she had said all this in a rush, she plumped back down again.

"Aaaaa—that's what I really wanted to say at the meeting yesterday. Hey, give me some tea too," she added hastily, pointing to the cup from which I was drinking.

"But you know what made me glad? (Mom drank down the tea with a loud gulp.) Those fathers, I don't know who they are or where they live, about three of them, said some very good things. Tommy, I bet you would have thought so too if you'd been there. Ah, well, no, not you. But men—you can count on them."

From the time I was five Mom, never remarrying, brought me up on the meager estate Dad left behind, which might be why she looks for heroism in men.

It's not that I don't like to see Mom's beaming face, but when she gets too full of herself, I don't like it. When she fails to say what she wanted to say and thumps back down into the kitchen chair, that's not bad.

When I was little, I used to go outside every evening and gaze at the great sun setting in the west.

"Please, when the sun sets today, let the sky be clear. Or if not, let the rain come pouring down."

Of course I still remember Mom's inconsolably sad face in those days when she would go out on the balcony every morning and pray to the sky.

It's true still today, but in those days my love of sunsets was famous. While all the light in the world was bundled to dye the sky ruby red, I would go into a trance-like state, and stand motionless to the end. No matter who called me, no matter what happened, until the last golden ray dropped away as if pulled by something, and pure darkness spread luxuriantly, I just stared at the sky.

But that was when the sky was clear. If any clouds appeared and obstructed the sun, havoc began. I would cry as if to burst my throat, besieged by a terror as if the world were coming to an end.

Only crying and screaming could give me a measure of relief from the bottomless despair that possessed me.

On days when it was already raining I would resign myself. But when a lot of clouds were moving in a lot of different directions, then there was trouble.

I could accept it if the sun set behind something fixed, like a mountain, the horizon, or the roof of a building.

But when the floating clouds changing their shapes moment by moment—nothing threw me into greater anxiety.

Every time a cloud moved to hide the sun, I would let out a shriek that split the sky. No one could stop me.

To people from the neighborhood who came out to see what was going on or to passersby who stopped, Mom would say things like "He's just an unreasonable child," but even as she did so, she looked somehow valiant.

"If only we could have put your cries in a glass jar and preserved them. I could open them now and let you listen little by little. And what if some of that beautiful ruby red came floating out as well . . . ?"

Mom looked at me with faraway, slightly unfocused eyes.

But that's just what I am always thinking. I wish I could take all those various moments from the past that I love so well and that sustain me in the present, and put them into jars and line them up in my room.

For me who never thinks about the future, pulling the past little by little out of the corners of my memory is my daily work.

And if from those jars could come sounds, colors and smells, I can guarantee that my existence would become more real.

The funeral service for Mrs. Tōno was held at the Larkhill Community Center.

Mom set out early with Mrs. Kawabata, saying they were supposed to help out.

When I passed along the side of the hall, I looked in the window to see Mr. Tōno, a high-school boy, and a middle-school girl, all looking down.

The face in the photograph surrounded by chrysanthemums bore a very happy smile, which led me to think, though I don't understand these things very well, that compared to dying of sickness, maybe it's a happier thing to be killed.

That day I came home muttering, "When do you die?" over and over.

"You mean to say 'When do I die.' It's so simple. The distinction between yourself and others, why can't you get it? I've explained it to you time after time."

Just when I thought she was going to contort her face, she sat down and laid her head on the kitchen table. Maybe because of the funeral, Mom was a little more sentimental than usual. I also for some reason felt sad, and abandoning myself to the words that streamed from my lips, I went into my regular monologue.

When I came to myself, outside the windows was pitch dark. I turned on the light and looked into Mom's face, to find she was snoring slightly.

Maybe she sensed my movements because she suddenly raised her right hand and pointed at me, shouting, "Tonight is hamburgers! You're the chef!"

Actually I had been in the mood for meatballs, but hamburgers are also one of my specialties, so I thought, OK, I can live with that, and started to peel an onion.

"So was the killer really one of those people? At the funeral that's what everybody was whispering. 'Who else could it be?' Ah, I hate it! I hate it! For two years I've been sticking my neck out. Whenever the slightest bad rumor started around, there I was saying, 'Oh, no, it wasn't one of them.' Oh I wish they would hurry up and arrest somebody who has nothing to do with the workshop."

Mom looked terribly disheartened.

"Hey, you forgot garlic again—just because you don't like it yourself. But a little bit of garlic adds to the flavor."

Though she looked as though her mind were far away, evidently she was keeping a close watch on me, and sent out her "no-no" signal right on time.

Since the incident, a pair of policemen has been walking around the neighborhood every day.

And the patrolmen stationed at the police box at the entrance to our area also come into town often.

They say there are also policemen at the workshop, watching how the people there work and behave.

"I think it might be him. You know, that middle-aged man who comes in to the convenience store sometimes to shop. I wonder if he's on medication. He seems to be in a kind of a daze."

When Mom heard these words from a neighborhood woman, the pain showed in her face.

Two weeks have passed. The killer has still not been arrested.

The weather had been clear all week, but it is threatening to rain on the weekend. That's why Mom is nagging me with her tedious admonitions.

"Be careful, OK? Just deliver the newspaper right. Don't let them get wet again."

It's been about a year since I started delivering newspapers in Larkhill.

One rainy day when I had some twenty papers left in the basket, I was trying to turn the bike around and I skidded in a puddle, quite beautifully overturning the bike, papers and all. Of course, all the papers were soaked.

With that shock the hoop inside my head, which had been loose, tightened down.

I still had eighteen homes to deliver newspapers to. My brain quickly went into high gear. Desperately I tried to salvage the papers, but when I picked them up, they crumbled through my fingers.

Then I spotted a pile of newspapers tied up in the garage of the house right in front of me. They were under the roof, so they weren't wet.

"Yahoo!"

I untied the strings, put those papers in the basket, and delivered them to the last eighteen houses.

The dealer was flooded with angry phone calls. Mom had to visit each of the eighteen homes and offer abject apologies. Looking at me, who remained detached and nonchalant, she said,

"You are incredible," and took to her bed for two days.

I was told that those were old papers that had been tied up to give to the scrap-paper man, but I still think it was a brilliant idea to use them.

Ever since then Mom's hatred of early-morning rain has been quite something. She doesn't go so far as to go out on the balcony and say a prayer each morning like she used to, but she's very jumpy about the TV weather forecast.

Today it hasn't started to rain yet, but the moist morning breeze carries the scent of flowers.

I stop my bike, put in a paper, start pedaling again, stop again, put in another paper. Each time the mailbox lid flops shut, the sound it makes gives me indescribable joy.

There are different kinds of mailboxes. Some don't have hinged tops, while other houses have vinyl bags hung out for me to put the papers in, so I don't get that wonderful sound every time.

That makes me very unhappy, and to tell the truth I don't feel like delivering papers where I can't hear that sound, but I've recently been able to figure out that this is a job, and that I am to deliver the papers to those places too. But I don't want to see those mailboxes, so what I do is shut my eyes when I put the papers in them.

I went past a hedge, then a closed garage door, and put a paper in a long slim mailbox attached to the gate. Then a memory floated up in my mind.

Yes, it was Saturday two weeks ago, 4:52 am. I was working right on time.

Just when I put a paper in this box and began to pedal my bike, I heard a voice behind me, a gate opened, and a woman ran in the opposite direction as if escaping, with a boy of about high-school age running after her.

The reason I'm sure about the time is that every morning after I deliver the paper to that house on the corner, I look at my watch under the lamp at the gate.

Because of this obsession with time, which Mom describes as a fear akin to that of someone on death row, I always check the time no matter what happens. Other people will say, "Ah, it's morning, it must be time to get up," or "It's about time to leave." But for me it's not looking at the clock to see what time it is. It's time itself, as shown by the hands of the clock, that I cling to.

That's why every morning, looking at my watch after I deliver the paper to the house on the corner is a fixed rule.

If the time at this point is even slightly closer to 4:50 am my satisfaction level goes up, and if I am then able to get back home at exactly 5:30 am I know it's going to be a happy day.

The accuracy with which I can recall the dates and places of past events is virtually absolute.

This is one thing Mom really trusts me with, and when she wants to get some event straight she always asks me.

But what I remember is not significant world events or incidents memorable for the family, but things like when and where we had dinner with my aunt and cousins, and what we ate. Even if it was ten years ago I remember things like that exactly, which is why Mom asks me.

I guess Mom thinks remembering things like that is a waste of time.

But when relatives visit or when she is talking with friends, trivia questions like that come up, and she will suddenly ask,

"Tommy, when was that?"

And then when I tell her she says, as a conclusion,

"Oh yes, that's right, that's right."

Mom also has a bit of a desire to boast about my powers of memory, so she asks me questions like that pretty often.

That's how it is with me. The events of the past are organized in my memory along a time line, and so when some connection appears between an event of the past and what is happening in the present, the memory floats up in my mind.

That's why this time, the moment I put the paper in that long, slim mailbox, it came back to me. The scene in front of this house two weeks before. Down the quiet, deadly dark early morning road, the woman who came out of the gate, the young man, perhaps chasing her, disappear, running, in the distance. Stopping my bike at the street corner, I gaze fixedly at the two figures, whose limbs seem to move with an odd slowness as they melt into the darkness.

To tell the truth, while I was watching them I was pulling out a completely different memory from the past and spreading it out inside my head.

It's still true today, but when I was a child I loved long, dark holes.

Tunnels, manholes. At home, the toilet and the sink.

As I never think about or have any image of the future, perhaps dark holes were the only paths I could find that could link me to the unknown.

That day the dark road in front of the Tōno house appeared to me like a tunnel, and the sight of the two figures that seemed to be swimming down it ever farther away was so heartrending that my thoughts traveled back into the past.

One day when I was in the fourth grade I found an open manhole near my home. The earth around it had been excavated, so I could see the drainpipe attached to it.

For me, nothing could have been more intriguing. First I took a good, long look down the manhole, and then started walking along parallel to the drainpipe. A ditch had been dug from the manhole and new pipe was laid on the ground along it. I would crouch down, peer into one length of pipe, walk to the next one, and crouch down again.

In this way I advanced down the pipeline. It was just before sunset, my favorite time of day. As I walked along, before me was the great setting sun sending out its last bundle of rays that dyed the sky ruby everywhere you could see.

Then I noticed that the pipe, half buried in the earth, went into the garden of a house alongside the road. Quite naturally, I slipped in through the open gate. I came into a narrow space with a window on the other side. The pipe apparently went in under the floor. That seemed to be where my tunnel ended. Then I looked up, and saw framed in the window the figure of a woman taking a shower.

As I stood in awe, gray darkness gradually climbed from my feet up along my body. The light went on inside, melting into the steam and blurring the woman's figure.

While I watched, I became saturated with a splendidly comfortable feeling that I had never experienced before.

"Gyaaaa!"

There was a scream and a loud bang. The side door opened and a woman came out.

"The idea! Why? What a fright you gave me! What do you think you are doing? I won't forgive you just because you are a child."

In the darkness only her white gown floated before me.

"I wonder which tunnel the longest tunnel is."

Desperately I tried to communicate to her the supreme happiness I had been feeling.

The woman took a step back, then looked closely into my face.

"What's that? What's going on with you?" Her voice softened. Her question was not something she expected an answer to, but rather was intended to give her more time to look me over. She walked around me once, and then bent backward to have another look at my face.

While she did that I was gazing at the last ray of the sunset reflected on the roof behind her.

"Where do you live? What's your name?"

Her voice was calmer, but her exploring eyes still showed traces of anxiety.

"Now, look at that, you have a name tag on you. So you're a fourth-grader at the elementary school over there."

She looked into my face once again in the light coming from the doorway, and her expression finally relaxed.

"Don't ever do a thing like that again. Not ever!"

Having said that with a stern face, the woman disappeared inside.

The next day Mom, with an unusually gloomy look, grabbed me by my shoulders, sat me down in a chair, knelt on the floor in front of me and gazed into my face.

"A person who sneaks into someone else's house is called a thief. If you don't understand that, what is there to do?—you who are a fourth-grader now. It seems that someone from that house notified the school. I got a call from your teacher. If you keep on doing that kind of thing, I'll have to take you somewhere, no matter how much I'm your Mom."

Mom's eyes reddened.

I was flustered and thought I ought to say something, but I couldn't even come up with a question from my regular repertoire.

That evening's sunset, with the woman's body permeated and reflected in it, remains still today a treasure in my memory box.

But some official in that area's neighborhood association heard about the incident and wrote about it in the circular letter that gets passed from house to house. Mom heard about it from a friend who lives near there. It said,

"Recently a suspicious child seems to be loitering in our neighborhood, but on inquiring at his school we have determined that he poses no particular danger, so there is no need to be alarmed."

It seemed that Mom was more shocked to hear that than when she heard what I had done. I remember her crying loudly while vacuuming. Usually when Mom wants to cry, she starts vacuuming. The whine of the vacuum cleaner and the sound of her sobbing form a duet.

"'Presents no danger!' To say that about a ten-year-old child. It's an insult, talking about somebody else's child as if he were a monster!"

She was muttering and sobbing at the same time.

It turned out that what I had seen that morning had something to do with the murder. The police finally determined that Tōno had been killed by her high-school-age son.

"I hear he was a straight-A student. They say he was exhausted from too much studying for college entrance exams."

"And they say his mother was an Education Mama, and they were always quarreling."

"And that very morning too. I hear he had been up all night studying, and she started railing at him and that started a fight."

"But he sat right next to his father at the funeral. I wonder what was going on in his mind."

The neighborhood aunties never ran out of things to talk about.

"Well, thank goodness that's over. I'm so relieved it wasn't some-one from the workshop. But to be killed by your own son! Maybe it was better she died. To live all your life with the fact that your own son had stabbed you—that would be too painful for both of them."

Mom seemed to be gazing at something in the far distance. Her eyes were filled with a color of deep grief that I had never seen be-fore.

What is it? What is it? That sorrowful look had gotten hold of me. Unless I figured it out, I couldn't take one more step forward. I couldn't have today.

Completely absorbed, I began shaking loose the past that was packed in my head.

Dad was kind.

I was only five when he died, but in every scene I remember about him, he was kind.

I am sitting in the sandbox at the playground, enjoying the feel-ing of the sand sifting out of my hands, and he is sitting beside me, scooping up sand as well.

I am nothing if not persistent. Once I start a game like this I have no idea how to stop.

Whether the children around me are capering, crying, or laugh-ing has absolutely nothing to do with me. Single-mindedly I go on scooping my sand and letting it slip gently through my fingers.

The feel of the sand sliding across the soft skin of my fingers gives me almost unbearable pleasure.

If I am interrupted, I start screeching.

This sand play may go on for an hour or two hours, until some chance brings me to my feet.

And then I break into a run.

Dad rushes after me and picks me up, but I bend backward in his arms, and never nestle my head against his chest.

That wasn't because it was Dad; from the time I was a baby, I've never understood what it is to cuddle up to someone.

I live willfully, following the sensations that flash inside my head. And so I'm also quite sensitive to the shifts in the feelings toward me of the people around me. With the accumulated memories of these things as my center, I live in the present.

The fact that I didn't like to be held by Dad or hold hands with him didn't mean I rejected him. Rather, some incomprehensible thing in my nature made me act that way.

For all that, Dad was always kind to me. It's even sad, how kind he was.

My love of dark holes began around then.

Those two little holes in the middle of people's faces. My interest in them made me awkward to deal with.

Whenever I met someone I wanted to look at the holes in their nose, and so no matter who it was I would go up to touch their face.

My victims tended to be little children because of their small size.

When I would pinch and peek into the nose of a baby in a carriage, that was trouble.

I moved quickly, and Dad would get all upset racing after me; when he bowed in apology his figure looked somehow small and forlorn.

It was also Dad who would read me my favorite children's book, *Rice Balls, Kororin*.

"Once upon a time a very diligent and right-minded old man . . ."

As if prompted by his voice, I tip-tap on the book. It means he should read on quickly.

My goal is to get to the double-spread picture on pages 3 and 4, showing mice in their mouse hole, all surrounded by black.

"Every time the old man sent a rice ball tumbling *kororin kororin* into the dark hole, he would hear a clear voice from below saying, "*kororin! kororin!*" The old man got so curious that finally he went tumbling *kororin* into the hole himself . . ."

At the top of the picture there is a round blue sky, and right in the middle of the black below that, the old man's legs in red trousers and straw sandals leap out at me.

When we reach that point my body stiffens, I hold my breath a moment, then burst out laughing.

A bashful smile spreads over Dad's face, and he holds me tight.

His body had a slightly oily smell. I can still remember it clearly. I'm almost there.

That terribly sad look on Mom's face, that complex expression I had never seen before, when she learned that Mrs. Tōno had been killed by her own son—I'm getting close to its source.

I have the feeling there is a page in my memory box that is impatiently waiting for its cue to come popping out.

I was riding in a car.

Dad was driving. For some reason, Mom was not with us. The sky spread out in endless blue.

"Tommy, is this the first time just the two of us have taken a drive together?"

Dad, a man of few words, spoke as if he were measuring my mood.

I loved cars, so I was thoroughly enjoying myself without thinking about him.

But the strange thing was, I was in the back seat instead of in the passenger seat where I always sat. Since I loved riding in the car so much it was a fixed matter that when the three of us went for a drive I would sit in front and Mom in back.

So why on earth was I in back? Obsessive as I am, I must have put up quite a fight.

"After we get over this hill, there's a place where they serve very good omelets. You like omelets, don't you Tommy?"

With Dad at the wheel, the car went up the mountain road, swaying from left to right.

The omelet I had was very good.

Under the pale, yellow skin pulpy onion, permeated with the smell of butter, was waiting for me.

Dad drank a beer as he watched me shoveling the food into my mouth.

"All right, let's go."

He got up slowly and turned toward me. His face was a little red, and his eyes seemed misty.

And that was the end. The next page in my memory box had remained closed. Until today.

Dad is dead. He was driving, and now he is dead. Dad is dead. Dead . . . like an echo these words race around in my head.

"Tommy! Tommy!"

As I woke up I seemed to hear Mom's voice calling me. Everything around me is white. In the middle of the white, Mom's face is gazing at me.

My head hurt. I tried to move my hands but they wouldn't obey, as if they had been tied down. There were tubes going into my nose and arms.

"Ah, good. At least Tommy will live."

Her weeping voice broke.

So that's how it was. Dad had wanted to die with me. But I survived.

He crashed the car into a rock, so if I had been sitting in the front I definitely would have been killed.

But he didn't seat me there. It was, at the final moment, Dad's kindness.

Now, after twenty-five years I have linked my memories together.

But I don't have the courage to tell Mom that I have figured it out.

To begin with, I still haven't found the *language* I could use to say it to her.

6

TOMMY'S SUNSET

Mom isn't back yet.

I'm sure it was 9:10 in the morning when she left. She said she wanted to catch the 9:18 bus and went out in a hurry.

"I think I'll be back around two. Don't worry about dinner. I'll cook you something." She had closed the front door, but opened it again from outside and said this without looking at me.

Now four hours had passed since two o'clock. I went outside.

Though I wasn't thinking at all about sunsets today, I was welcomed by the huge orange sphere burning beyond the road.

Abruptly a black hand reached out from the side. Unconsciously I ducked my head to dodge—a crow.

The bird had taken off from our neighbor's roof and darted across the setting sun.

It's unusual for me, but today I was in the house all day long. And yet Mom didn't even call. She told me she was going to the hospital.

Breast cancer, I guess, is a pretty difficult illness.

Yes, it was just a week ago on Monday that Mom had a panic attack, a Big Bang that violently shook the whole house.

On the day before that we had some calm ordinary moments together, which started with my words, *at the age of sixty-two.*

Now I think there was definitely something in those moments that presaged Monday's Big Bang.

"I wonder what will happen at the age of sixty-two."

I had no idea where I had gotten the idea of an age of sixty-two. Mom, in front of her mirror, was closing her eyes and pinching her cheeks, but turned her head in my direction.

"Huh? Who's sixty-two?" she asked. "Hey, who are you talking about?"

The generous sun was still pouring light diagonally through the windowpanes. It was a mild morning.

"When do you die?" I mumbled.

"Humph," Mom snorted. "Aaaaaa, pitiful, pitiful. At the age of thirty. That 'you' you said just now means me, that is, Mom. Because there's only the two of us here."

She made her usual comment and turned back to the mirror.

In the mirror I saw a smile flicker in her eyes.

"But in your case it's different. When you say 'you' you mean 'I.' So just now you asked when *you* will die, right?"

Since Mom was speaking while putting lipstick on her upper lip, her words were not too clear.

"At sixty-two, maybe dead?"

"What?"

She turned to me. The lipstick had slipped over the upper lip and the pale lower lip looked somehow eerie. Holding her lipstick, Mom let her eyes swim this way and that.

"Well . . . forget it. It just tires me out if I take what you say seriously."

She returned to the mirror.

"Oh, I see. You were talking about the time when you get to be sixty-two. I get it."

Having lived with a son like me for thirty years, Mom is very good at convincing herself.

Her face came out from inside the mirror and approached me.

"And then I will be eighty-eight! Wow, that's thirty years from now. No, I won't be dead. How could this Mom ever die?!"

A large mouth opened before me.

"I wonder what's for dinner tonight."

I asked the thing I had been worrying about.

"That's not the thing to say now."

Mom went brusquely to the window.

"Well, I have a dream. It's to go to live in a nice nursing home with Tommy."

"I wonder where the nursing home . . . is. Where?"

Occasionally I manage really to talk to Mom. And if she's going to talk about us entering a nursing home . . . !

Perhaps pleased with my reaction, she raised her voice.

"See, see, Tommy? You react nicely if it's something directly related to you."

She picked up her hairbrush and busied herself with her hair.

"These days, you know, we hear all the time about husbands and wives moving into nursing homes together—it's so tacky. Wouldn't it be cool for a parent and child to move in?"

Why do we have to move into a place like that? No matter how old I get, I want to live in this house in Larkhill—even if I'm alone. That's what I thought.

It's Mom who always says, *We've got to be independent of each other. You mustn't cling to me forever.* And now she's talking about us living together in an old people's home.

Evidently my feelings got transmitted to her.

"Yes, it'd be odd. Well, we don't have to go to a nursing home. We can stay in this house till the end, can't we?"

Mom nodded to herself.

"But . . ."

Back in the mirror, her eyeballs moved diagonally, then halted.

"But I wonder if you were talking about me at sixty-two."

Her face in the mirror looked smaller than life.

"If it's about me, I'll be sixty-two four years from now. If I'm dead then, we can't meet any more, Tommy. Is it all right to talk lightly about such things?"

"What happens when you're dead?"

"When a person is dead, they're nowhere at all, no matter where you look."

"What about the funeral?"

". . . Stop that. Why is it only to subjects like this that you react so quickly?"

From time to time, funerals are held at Larkhill Community Center.

Since many years ago, I find myself in good spirits when things are precisely scheduled. And if things actually follow that schedule, I become happier still. Therefore it would be better if the day, month, and year of Mom's funeral were already set.

Enough of your company is enough. Her face saying so, she left the room.

That was an easy, ordinary conversation between Mom and me about something that had to occur someday in the future but not necessarily today or tomorrow.

The next day she went to have her annual checkup with her friend Mrs. Kawabata.

They returned after three hours or so, took seats in the kitchen, and talked about the lunch they had eaten at the Woodpecker restaurant.

Mom picked up a dishcloth and kept busily wiping the table, though it wasn't dirty at all.

"Don't you think it was better before?"

"Well . . ."

"Maybe they have a new chef. The sauce tasted different."

"Maybe so."

Only Mrs. Kawabata talked and Mom remained passive. Mom's voice was somehow different from usual.

After folding the cloth neat and tight, she spoke as though she had made up her mind about something.

"This time I have the feeling it's not going to be all right."

"Hey, hey. Don't worry. Lots of people are asked to have another test. You'll see. *There's nothing wrong with you. Come back next year.* That'll be it."

Mrs. Kawabata's rebuttal sounded as though she had anticipated what Mom was going to say.

I was sitting at the same table with them and helping myself to cookies, but to them I was merely part of the scenery.

"You know, this is the third year in a row I have received a warning. I hate to be tested again."

Without looking at Mrs. Kawabata's face, she started wiping the table again—wiping, that is, only moving the cloth back and forth across the same place in front of her.

"Even supposing you do have it, breast cancer is so common these days. You have an operation and that's the end of it."

Mrs. Kawabata picked up one of the cookies that were in front of me and put it into her mouth.

Both fell silent for a while.

"I wonder how old Mrs. Kawabata is."

I asked this because Mom's unprecedented mood made me feel insecure. Though I was worrying so hard about Mom, what she would call irrelevant words came out.

They ignored me and went on talking.

"If it's breast cancer, suppose it's already spread? I'd be hit harder than when I listened to that doctor explain about Tommy twenty-five years ago, and it sank in that he would be just like this all his life."

Mrs. Kawabata's munching sounds stopped.

"You know misfortune multiplied by misfortune is double misfortune. Tommy depends on me like this, and he already has his misfortune, which makes him suffer triple misfortune. Plus, his father is dead, so he's loaded with quadruple misfortune. What if I have to leave him like that . . . ?"

Mom, half frantic with despair, was just putting her overflowing emotions into words.

"What time is it? What time is it?" It was unbearable, so I asked this.

"Oh my, it's so late!"

Mrs. Kawabata, apparently relieved, looked at the wall clock and got to her feet.

"This is ridiculous! Oh, yes, indeed you are the most unfortunate human being in the world. Poor you. Anyway, don't jump to any conclusions. You'll know after the work-up the day after tomorrow. I'm one hundred percent sure you'll be all right."

"I wonder what day of the week the day after tomorrow will be."

I tried to encourage Mom by posing my pet question, but she again failed to respond with her rubber stamp, "*Again you say such an irrelevant thing!*"

"I'm sorry, I shouldn't have kept you so long."

Speaking in a voice a number of times softer than usual, Mom saw Mrs. Kawabata off.

I now think the whole thing began with my words—*I wonder what will happen at the age of sixty-two.*

Two days later, after coming home from her reexamination, Mom went into the kitchen without a word and opened the refrigerator. Her head and shoulders formed a fragile silhouette against its inside light. The silhouette began to move little by little.

If I open the refrigerator and leave it open while I hesitate about what to take out, Mom is sure to scream, *Hurry up and shut the door!*

Broken sobs rose together with the sound of the closing door. Mom turned toward me, her face twisted with pain.

"Tomio, Tomio."

Calling out my real name, she wept aloud.

Even when I was seriously injured in the road accident, she wasn't like this. Whatever happened, once the first impact subsided she could always bring out a new light from her hands—like a magician who opens his hands and lets fly a dove.

I could do nothing but keep standing still.

Her body shaking, she sat in a chair. Then she went face-flat on the table. Suddenly I wanted to eat something and opened the refrigerator. I thought of steaming some Chinese pork buns. I put water into a pot and placed it over the gas. White clouds of steam started rising from around the lid. Watching this, I somehow began to feel sad.

I put a steaming bun on a plate and put it by Mom's head.

"Pork bun, pork bun."

Hearing my voice, Mom slowly raised her face, grimaced, then went to the sink. I rolled the other bun in my hands, blew on it, and ate it.

After Mom washed the makeup off her face, her eyes looked red and swollen.

She sat on the chair and, hiccupping, said, "Rising steam is nice, isn't it?"

Pressing her left hand to her eyes, she munched her bun and sniffled.

"I have cancer. Breast cancer. You may not understand very well, but it's quite a serious illness. Today the doctor told me. He had suggested that I bring a family member with me, but what could I do? I said I would be all right, and went by myself to hear what he had to say."

She paused. "I'm sorry I didn't treat you as a family member."

Perhaps she had run out of tears, for though she sniffled at times, the usual Mom was coming back by bits and pieces.

"Having said that, I wonder what 'family' means."

She was stumbling over her own words.

"You don't do this often, but just now you took the trouble to steam pork buns and bring one for me, and it's only Tommy that I don't mind showing my face to without makeup like this. But in the eyes of people in the world, particularly when a decision has to be made for someone, Tommy doesn't qualify as family. But I, your mother, shouldn't be the first to accept that . . ."

"I wonder when you go into the hospital. I wonder what day next week it will be."

As to staying in the hospital, I was Mom's senior. I was recalling the long days that I had spent in the hospital because of the accident.

"They say if you confide your troubles to someone you'll feel yourself cleared up, but then I worry about how that someone might think about it later, and how I might regret having spoken. But with you I can feel at ease. You are like water, where I can see a reflection of my heart, and there it ends."

Mom said this much, and pulled the string to turn on the light. Without our noticing, it had grown dark outside.

"This is too bright."

She pulled the string again to tone down the light.

"See? It's here, breast cancer."

She had risen to her feet and made toward the sink, but then surprised me by turning around with her hand on a breast.

"Since I was told about it, I don't know why but it's like all my nerves have converged in this breast. To think that something repulsive is living in here. The other day you asked, 'When do you die?' That was definitely about me after all. The age of sixty-two sounds all too realistic. I'm fifty-eight now. But no, you couldn't have said such a thing in earnest. I'm sure I'll be all right. I'll live on until you reach the age of sixty-two, you'll see!"

Mom took out the cutting board and started chopping leeks.

"I'll ask Aunt Tanabe to come tomorrow."

Aunt Tanabe is Mom's younger sister who lives about forty minutes away by train.

"There are many things I want to explain to her. You're always asking about someone dying, aren't you? It may be my turn."

The end of her last sentence was quivering. It gave me a hunch that maybe her Big Bang wasn't over yet.

She had said she would live until I was sixty-two, and then that she'd be dead at sixty-two. I wondered what was going on in her head.

Aunt Tanabe came.

She welcomes me whenever I visit her on my own, and kindly makes my favorite *okonomiyaki* pancakes—my only relative in the world. Apparently Mom had already talked to her on the phone, for she came to my side as soon as she entered the room and knowingly looked into me with her big eyes that don't resemble Mom's at all.

"Tommy, you look well. You'll be fine, won't you? I'll think about it, just how we can manage things . . ." Her eyes were on Mom while she spoke.

Why are they busying themselves with things about me as a problem because Mom got sick? If she goes into the hospital, I'll do my paper route as usual, make sandwiches or cook fried rice, and go to bed by myself. To worry more about a healthy person like me than about Mom who is sick seems strange.

Maybe because of the immediate family affection Mom was accepting whatever Aunt Tanabe said or did. Vaguely I felt lonesome.

"You have to conquer it and that's the first thing. Tommy will be all right."

"Yes, we'll find a way. Tommy and I haven't survived these thirty years for nothing."

Yes, that's vintage Mom. She does tend to brag a little. But when night came she would suffer a big relapse. I was not yet aware of that part of the Big Bang waiting deep inside her.

The next push came after Aunt Tanabe left, when Mom was attacked from a different direction.

A young woman visited us in the evening, holding a baby in her arms.

"He is your son, isn't he?"

The woman recognized me when I came with Mom to the entrance hall. Mom acknowledged this with a smile on her face.

"The trouble is, it's so early in the morning. Your son passes our house mumbling along. So each morning my little girl wakes up and cries." Rocking her baby, she complained to Mom. Mom glanced at me and replied, "He goes on a paper route every morning. I guess he does his monologue when he passes your house. I am very sorry."

"I know he's delivering papers. But my baby is asleep in the house and it's a problem for us."

"If you say it's a problem for you, I can tell him to be careful, but he is as he is, so I can't just say, 'Yes, yes, I understand.' I am really sorry."

"Maybe for someone like him, holding a job is too much to expect. There are other things . . ."

"Well, it seems they can't find many people to do deliveries in the early hours. They say my son is helpful and he's been at it a long time."

"But to be honest, it's a nuisance."

"Who is it? Who is it?"

I said this not for myself but because I felt Mom might start crying again.

"I am sorry. But isn't he near your place only for a minute or two? I think there are other noises as well—sounds from motorbikes and dogs barking."

Predictably, Mom's voice gradually lowered.

"I wonder if the moon is full or crescent tonight."

I said this in a loud voice. The baby in the woman's arms looked at me with wide-open eyes.

"Please think about it; you're his mother. I can't tell him to stop it."

The woman had also lost her initial edge. She left, dandling her child who had gotten fractious.

Mom heaved a sigh. There were dark rings around her eyes and only her eyeballs were luminous.

"She said, 'Maybe for someone like him, holding a job is too much to expect.' She was talking about you, Tommy. She said you shouldn't have a job. Anyway, don't talk to yourself."

"I wonder how the moon is tonight."

"Hey, suppose we sent out a questionnaire about this to the people in the neighborhood. Which do you think they would support— her or me? Which would be the majority?"

Mom's eyes, which had been on the verge of crying, now smiled a little and the last question was pronounced in rhythm.

"Her, of course. Because it's about her pretty baby. Because her baby can't sleep. In contrast, look at you. A bearded thirty-year-old soliloquist who doesn't make any sense."

Tears started rolling down again and got tangled with two or three strands of her hair. I had never seen Mom cry like this. It must have been because of that checkup. It must have been because of her breast cancer.

"But you'd never find another job if you quit the paper route now. What can I do? So you can truly live . . ."

Mom spent the rest of the night in silence. After dinner she cleared the table in her usual way, then sat before the television busily changing channels. Usually she would check the newspaper's TV page, find an old Western movie, and sit down happily. But not today. She didn't seem to care at all about what was on.

A man and a woman were on the screen, talking about something. After a while the woman began to cry and tried to fight back her sobs. Then there was another scene in which two women were laughing with their mouths open wide. Nevertheless I heard sobs. I had thought they came from the tube, but it was Mom who was crying.

Whatever scenes came up on the screen, her subdued weeping didn't stop. In contrast with those loud cries in front of the refriger-

ator that had astounded me, these soft, deep sobs seemed to be coming out of a sadness in the furthest reaches of her heart.

Breast cancer must be an awfully difficult illness. Mom said she
might die from it. Is she going to die? To die means a person is
nowhere to be found.

On the television, the sun was setting over the edge of a mountain. It's the sunset I love so much. When I was very young, I made
it a rule to take my bath in the evening, just as the sun was setting.
That was one of my obsessions then.

Winter or summer, from the time the sun began to set and the sky
was turning ruby red until it got dark, that was when I was in the bath.
If this chance was missed, I wouldn't budge an inch. A cloudy sky in
the evening made me saddest of all. I remember a period in my life
when every evening I would go outside and never tired of watching
the sky. If the sky was filled with clouds I would resign myself. But
when clouds were floating separately, that was awful. I would cry
loudly each time the sun went behind a cloud. That was because just
when I thought the sun had reappeared, it disappeared again.

At those times, Mom would walk around me and seemed to share
my tears. I soon noticed that a sheaf of light rays would fleetingly
move each time the sun went behind a cloud or got clear of it. During that superlative time of day, I took to taking a bath with her.

Those ruby skies that I watched through the small window in the
bathroom still linger in my heart.

In the pauses in the sound from the television, I could hear
Mom's feeble voice.

That's it. *Everyone who is dead is on the other side of the setting
sun*—this notion began to grow inside me.

"Where—I wonder where the setting sun goes."

*Stop crying, Mom. When you die, you can be by the evening sun
that I love so well. It's all right, Mom. You can go there and I can go
there too. You told me before—that everyone is going to die. Even if
everybody in the world dies, there's no need to worry, because the sun is
so big. It's going to be all right.* (I was shouting in my heart.) *So please
stop crying.*

"I wonder where the setting sun goes," I said once again.

"The sun—your favorite sun—it sets in the west. As you know from long ago."

Mom's teary voice laughed for a fleeting second.

"Really, you and the setting sun are inseparable. That gave me such a lot of trouble."

Her voice became slightly upbeat.

"I won't cry any more. I can't make any sense of it, but for me, for you, I've shed enough tears. I feel like all the tears from my thirty years with you have come streaming out."

Mom told me to bring a can of beer and two tumblers.

"Shall we raise a toast? May Tommy live peacefully as he has, even if Mom is not around."

I was thinking: If Mom absolutely has to die, I pray she reaches the sun safely.

The next day, a city official came. It seems Mom had called the welfare section yesterday.

He produced documents from his bag and picked up his pen.

"You will be in hospital . . . from?"

"The date will be set when I go there tomorrow."

"And . . . Tomio-kun?"

He slightly raised his glasses and looked toward me.

"What about him when you are away?"

Looking at Mom and me in turns, he put the question to her. Even though she is the one who is ill and going into the hospital, everyone is worrying about me.

"Here are leaflets on some of the city facilities. I brought these because they have vacancies," he said, showing her several sheets of paper.

"They are more or less the same. He could stay until you leave the hospital, and if the worst happens, of course . . . Then again, even after you come home, he could stay as long as you might want him to."

It was just like the time someone from the post office came and tried to talk her into some insurance and installment savings plan.

I felt an unknown, burning power welling up inside me.

"I want to be in the house in Larkhill!"

These words jumped out of my mouth.

"Huh?"

It was Mom who turned around with an incredulous look. The official smiled leisurely and looked at her.

"This may be a good time for him to move in. You're lucky that there happen to be vacancies right now. Not many people leave these places once they are admitted."

A tinge of red appeared on Mom's cheeks. After days of being away, Mom was back.

"Did you hear what he said just now? Tomio said he wants to stay in this house in Larkhill."

The official silently looked at her.

"He goes on a paper route every morning and our neighbors understand about him. Just because I'll be in the hospital, to change his way of life . . ."

"Oh, no, of course we won't force you. But just in case, a lot of people are admitted while they are young, because their parents want to avoid trouble and confusion when the time finally comes."

He was pressing Mom while carefully watching her facial expressions.

"Anyway I will leave these leaflets with you. When you make up your mind, please let us know as soon as possible." He rose halfway to his feet, but suddenly bent over, his face contorted. "I have a strained back."

"My, my, that's too bad." Mom's voice sounded gleeful.

After she saw the strained-back off and shut the front door with a bang, she ran back to the sofa and sat beside me.

"More pain to you, Mr. Strainedback. Tommy, are you all right?"

Mom placed her hand on my brow and looked into my eyes.

"That was your once-in-a-lifetime, first-time-ever moment when you truly spoke your mind. *I want to be in the house in Larkhill.*"

Saying so, Mom covered her face with both hands and started to cry. She soon stopped, and took my hand with hers that was soaked with tears. Then she began to speak in an oddly high voice.

"Tommy, you've made me so happy. Yes, you *are* family. Tommy and I are a family. Just because one person in a family gets sick, the other doesn't have to leave home. Until I come back, you can live just as usual. Otherwise I can't be at ease in the hospital. He said, just in case and to avoid confusion. I think 'just in case' is what life is all about. If you aren't confused when someone is ill or someone dies, what then? If you want to avoid confusion, why not have everyone stay in the hospital forever from the day they're born? Confusion means you are truly alive. Things are all right as long as you have other people who support you when the confusion comes. So you can stay in this house as always, someone from the city office should come here to help you when something crops up that you can't do or have difficulty with, maybe an hour a day. It's that simple. I'll talk to the city office. Nothing could be simpler . . ."

Suddenly her voice died out. I wondered if she had fallen asleep, weary from talking too much.

Her head was thrown back on the sofa, her arms drooping, her eyes closed, her cheeks livid and hollow in ways I had never seen.

"I wonder what day of the week tomorrow will be."

I said this at the top of my voice. Her eyes partly opened.

"Hmm, Tommy, what happened? I turned faint? I wonder if it's anemia?"

That was last night.

Mom was still nowhere to be seen. I was standing in the street, face to face with the setting sun. It sank beyond the road, pouring its final-moment orange all around. At that moment I saw in the distance a car approaching as if it had loomed up from the ground. Its roof sign told me it was a taxi.

As I watched, the car pulled up beside me. Mrs. Kawabata got out and waved me to her.

"They decided to do the operation immediately. It starts in an hour or so. I'm on my way to the hospital. You come with me, Tommy."

I came back to her after locking the front door. "You've checked the gas, haven't you?" After confirming that, she said, "Hurry."

It was already pitch dark outside the windows of the car. We worked our way through several traffic jams and arrived at the hospital. Aunt Tanabe was already there.

We were sitting on a couch by the wall of a hall, when Mom appeared on a gurney with about three IV bottles attached to her. The three of us jumped to our feet like figures from a jack-in-the-box and looked down at her. She was already going into sleep.

"When do you die?"

I said this to Mom's face in a loud voice. A nurse glared at me.

I felt as though Mom smiled faintly.

The gurney wheeled ahead and was swallowed up by a white door.

Mrs. Kawabata and Aunt Tanabe were holding down my arms.

"What's on the other side of the sunset!?"

I shouted with all the strength of my body.

ABOUT THE AUTHOR

Hisako Tsurushima was born in Osaka in 1934. She began writing fiction when she entered Jyakucho Setouchi's writing school in 1985.

As her younger son with autism attended public elementary and middle schools, she organized a campaign for the inclusion of students with disabilities in public high schools and in community life. Now her son has a job working three days a week in the Hirakata city office.